ABOUT THIS BOOK

Welcome to Havenwood Falls, a small town in the majestic mountains of Colorado. A town where legacies began centuries ago, bloodlines run deep, and dark secrets abound. A town where nobody is what you think, where truths pose as lies, and where myths blend with reality. A place where everyone has a story. Including the high schoolers. This is only but one . . .

More than any other aspect of high school, Mallory Dorian dislikes most the mean girls. Every school has them, and her new school, Havenwood Falls High, is no exception. Beautiful. Fearless. Popular. They are the kind of girls everyone envies but secretly hates. Why they decide to make Mallory's life a living hell, she can't figure out. Maybe she looked at one of them wrong. Maybe she took away all the attention, being the new girl. Or maybe it's because she is falling for one of their boyfriends—Torent Stark, the mysterious and troublesome guy whom she can't seem to get out of her head.

Take your pick.

It doesn't matter.

What does matter is she's a threat they're determined to obliterate. But Mallory has her own problems. From the moment she stepped foot into the quaint mountain town, something has awakened inside her. Something she's never felt before and can't define. The mystic and dark waters call to her, beckoning her to discover her true self. But to find out what she is, Mallory must first survive her initiation into Havenwood Falls High.

HAVENWOOD FALLS HIGH BOOKS

Written in the Stars by Kallie Ross

Reawakened by Morgan Wylie

The Fall by Kristen Yard

Somewhere Within by Amy Hale

Awaken the Soul by Michele G. Miller

Bound by Shadows by Cameo Renae

Fata Morgana by E.J. Fechenda

Forever Emeline by Katie M. John

Reclamation by AnnaLisa Grant

Avenoir by Daniele Lanzarotta

Avenge the Heart by Michele G. Miller

Curse the Night by R.K. Ryals

Blood & Iron by Amy Hale

Shadows & Spells by Cameo Renae

Falling Deep by J.L. Weil

Saving Infiniti by Rose Garcia

Willful by Liz Ferry

Cast in Moonlight by Ali Winters

Promise the Moon by Kallie Ross

Blurred Lines by Daniele Lanzarotta

Ascending Darkness by J.L. Weil

Finding Infiniti by Rose Garcia

Unicorn's Lament by Megan Linski

Paper Bird by Amy Richie

Predestined by Valia Lind

Rediscovered by Morgan Wylie

Ashes of Fate by Apryl Baker

Stay up to date at www.HavenwoodFalls.com

ALSO BY J.L. WEIL

DRAGON DESCENDENTS SERIES

(Upper Teen Reverse Harem Fantasy)

Stealing Tranquility

THE DIVISA SERIES

(Full series completed – Teen Paranormal Romance)

Losing Emma: A Divisa novella

Saving Angel

Hunting Angel

Breaking Emma: A Divisa novella

Chasing Angel

Loving Angel

Redeeming Angel

LUMINESCENCE SERIES

(Full series completed – Teen Paranormal Romance)

Luminescence

Amethyst Tears

Moondust

Darkmist – A Luminescence novella

RAVEN SERIES

(Full series completed – Teen Paranormal Romance)

White Raven

Black Crow

Soul Symmetry

BEAUTY NEVER DIES CHRONICLES

(Teen Dystopian Romance)

Slumber

Entangled

Forsaken

NINE TAILS SERIES

(Teen Paranormal Romance)

First Shift

Storm Shift

Flame Shift

Time Shift

SINGLE NOVELS

Starbound

Casting Dreams

Ancient Tides

FALLING DEEP

A HAVENWOOD FALLS HIGH NOVELLA

J.L. WEIL

For all the girls who'd rather stay home and read than go to homecoming.

CHAPTER 1

$\mathcal{I}$ glanced in my rearview mirror, positive I was being punked. Nope. The boxes were still piled into the backseat of my aging Chevy Malibu. Forget trying to see out the back window. I had my whole life packed up in this hunk of junk.

Kind of sad.

Then again, my life was sad.

I was moving, leaving behind yet another house, another school, and another group of friends.

One year, I told myself. I only had one year left until I graduated, and then I could go wherever I wanted—live the life I chose—go to whatever college would have me. I only prayed this move didn't mess up my chances of getting a swimming scholarship.

I had worked too damn hard at being the best on my team. Correction—*had* been the best, but now that I was gone, the title went to Tiffany Hastings.

My fingers clenched on the wheel.

I'd miss a lot of things about living in Wisconsin, but Tiffany Hastings was definitely not one of them.

In a way, I was glad we were moving if it meant I would never again have to see Brady Cooper, the miserable bum Mom had been married to for the last two years. I wasn't going to miss his sorry face.

Mom had just signed the divorce papers from her third husband. Yep. Third. She wasn't lucky in love, or maybe it was because she only dated douchebags. And before the ink was even dry on the paper, Mom and I had our entire lives jammed into two cars, heading across the country to live in Havenwood Falls with my grandma, whom I called Gigi.

The town's stacked stone sign sat nestled between two flowering bushes, inviting and so cliché. I sank deeper into my seat, feeling anything but warm and fuzzy. "Welcome to Havenwood Falls" was written in black metal lettering.

I snorted. Welcome my left butt cheek. Finding this place had been a joke. I had nearly tossed the GPS out the window after the fourth time it tried to get me to turn around back the way I'd come.

Fortunately for us, Mom had been born here, yet still her sense of direction was crap. It was a freaking miracle we made it at all.

Let the suckage begin.

As I was reciting a list of things I already hated about Havenwood Falls, a streak of black darted out in front of my car, and reflexes kicked in as I slammed my foot on the brake. My poor car started to fishtail, and I knew this wasn't going to end well for either of us—the car or me.

I got one good glimpse of the creature before my car started to spin like a Ferris wheel on crack, and it didn't stop until the Malibu hit the ditch, snapping my head back against the seat.

Son of a—

God, that hurt.

I rubbed the back of my head, praying there was no blood. The last thing I needed was to pass out, and the sight of the metallic sticky stuff would do just that. I could handle lots of things—brussels sprouts, unnatural blondes, guys in thongs—but blood? Nope, no way.

My eyes flew out the window as I suddenly remembered the animal. I searched the road, looking for any sign of the critter. Had I hit it? Was it injured and lying hurt on the side of the street? Was I an animal killer?

Ensue panic attack.

I might be a lot of things, including the new girl, but I was definitely not a murderer.

But it was gone. Just vanished. My best guess? It had taken off into the woods after its brush with death.

Exhaling, I shifted the car into park and got out to check for damage. It wouldn't be the first mishap or dent Betsy had suffered. Betsy was what I called this piece of crap car. A few more dings would probably be an improvement, but really, I shouldn't complain. At least I had wheels to get me around. Not every seventeen-year-old could say the same.

As I glared down the road leading into Havenwood Falls, I realized Mom hadn't even stopped. Go figure. It would probably be a mile or more before she noticed I wasn't trailing behind her.

Fishing out my cell phone from the passenger seat, I sank back into the driver's seat and dialed her number. I left the door open, letting the crisp air of October rush over my face. She answered on the fifth ring.

"Hey, honey, you get lost?" Mom had a naturally husky voice that seemed to draw men to her like ants to a breadcrumb.

"Not exactly. I got run off the road."

"You what?" she shrieked in the shrill voice that always made me cringe. "By who? Another car?"

I rested my head on the back of the seat and closed my eyes for a moment. "Uh, no. It was an animal, I think. I'm going to need to call a tow truck."

"Are you okay at least?" she asked, suddenly getting around to worrying about my wellbeing. Mom wasn't what you would call responsible. She often forgot to turn off the coffee pot in the morning or pack my lunch when I was in first grade. I learned quickly how to take care of myself.

"I'm fine," I assured her. "Just another chapter to add to our adventure." Mom liked to think of each move—or *starting over,* as she so eloquently liked to say—as an adventure. I was tired of adventures and just wanted a place to call home.

"I'll turn around. Give me five minutes." Through the phone, I heard her flip on the blinker.

"Don't bother. I don't want to worry Gigi, and there's no need for us both to wait for someone to show up. I'll call you for directions as soon as my car is back on the road."

"Are you sure?"

"Positive. I'll just look up a towing company on my phone and give them a call. No big deal." So I kept telling myself. *I can handle this. It's time to start adulting.* Which I pretty much had been doing since I was ten. That was when husband number one had decided he'd had enough and split, walking out on us both.

I didn't know my real dad. Never had. One of the pitfalls of being a product of teen pregnancy. Eighteen-year-old prospective fathers don't always stick around.

We didn't need him.

"Okay, honey. Call me as soon as you're back on the road. The house is only ten minutes from where you are," she said. I could tell she was chewing on her lip, her nervous habit.

I assured her I would and hung up, immediately scouring the Internet on my phone for a local tow company. It took forever and a day for the search engine to load, and I blamed the soaring mountains. They were everywhere, and as breathtaking as the view was, my immediate concern was the crappy cell service.

"Come on," I encouraged under my breath, two seconds away from chucking my phone across the road. "Finally," I groaned as a single name and number popped up. *Havenwood Falls Garage & Tow Service.* Perfect. I clicked on the *Call Now* link and waited as the phone rang.

A gruff voice answered, and after I relayed my dire situation in way too much detail, he assured me help would be on the way in no more than twenty minutes. Crisis averted.

Now what to do to kill time? I tapped my fingers on the steering wheel before climbing out of the car. I left the keys in the cup holder and got my first real glimpse of the town I'd be living in for the next ten months. Come graduation, I was gone.

A river ran alongside the road near the base of the impressive mountains, bubbling faintly in the distance. The air was definitely crisp and cleaner as it moved in and out of my lungs. It seemed . . . peaceful, and I didn't know why that surprised me. Across the road was a quaint little neighborhood.

Pulling up the camera on my phone, I angled myself so the mountains were backdropped behind me and snapped a few selfies— okay, twenty, but I wanted to document the moment. My first catastrophe in my new home. Who wouldn't want that memory to laugh about someday?

I liked journals and scrapbooks. It was fun looking back on what was going on in my head or seeing the pictures of my friends. Wisconsin was far away now, including my old life. This marked my new journey aka stuck in hell, but regardless of the bad attitude, I would try for Gigi's sake to make the most of it. No moping around the house.

Fifteen minutes had passed when a truck pulled up, kicking dust in the air as I was snapping a picture of me in front of my poor car, angled so the trunk was sticking up in the air. I spun around and waited for the truck driver to get out. The name of the towing company was painted on the side of his cab. Tucking the loose strands of my honey-blond hair behind my ears, I smoothed the wrinkles from my hoodie. It had been a long drive, and I definitely wasn't looking my finest, but what did I care what some old grease monkey thought of me?

The door swung open and out stepped long legs covered in dark denim, but as the rest of him unfolded, my breath sort of stalled in my lungs. Broad shoulders lifted as he grabbed the side of the door, flashing a bit of defined abs. His jeans hung low on his hips, hugging a perfectly formed butt. My eyes traveled upward to his full, kissable lips, sharp cheeks, and stormy violet eyes fanned by sooty lashes. He looked down at me, the corner of his lip curving.

Holy crap. Nothing about the truck driver was greasy, saggy, smelly, or old.

5

His unusual and mesmerizing eyes captivated me, drawing me in until I felt as if I was floating in space.

Hot guy alert. Don't freak out. Don't freak out.

What did I do? I pocketed my phone and started rambling. "Thanks for coming. A thing jumped out in front of me, and I had to swerve off the road to avoid hitting it. Not exactly how I pictured my first day here, but maybe the universe is telling me something." *Someone stop me. Now! Before I give him my entire life story.*

"A thing?" he echoed in a deep, firm voice, lifting a condescending dark brow.

Internal wince. Hot guys made me nervous, and I couldn't be held accountable for the nonsense that came out of my mouth. "I'm not sure what it was—wolf or hellhound or bigfoot—take your pick. It was big and hairy."

His lips twitched. "If you say so."

A wave of embarrassment heated my cheeks.

He swept aside the half of his obsidian hair that was long, the other part shaved short. "Are the keys in the car?"

I nodded. "Cup holder."

He brushed past me to open the car door.

Damn. He smelled amazing, like insta-lust in a bottle.

I hated him. And wanted to have his babies at the same time.

"What are you doing in Havenwood Falls?" he asked as he dropped into the driver's seat, snatching up the keys. His eyes scanned the boxes in the backseat. "Vacation?"

"I wish," I groaned. "Divorce."

His questioning eyes found mine.

"Not me," I quickly clarified, feeling utterly mortified. "My mom. We're moving in with my grandma," I informed him, giving him more information than I normally would a total stranger.

"Sorry," he said, a glint of sympathy beaming in his gaze.

I hated being pitied, and my jaw tightened. "Nothing to be sorry for. Brady was a dick." Why was I telling him this?

"You should meet my brother. He takes being a dick to a new level."

I found my lips twitching, even though I didn't want to be amused by him. "And who would your brother be?" I fished. "Just so I can make sure to stay clear," I added so he wouldn't think I was hunting for information, which of course I was.

"I have two, but it's Brysen you have to watch out for. I'm Torent. Torent Stark. And you would be?" His smile reeked of trouble, and not the good kind.

"Mallory Dorian." I couldn't get over how perfectly symmetrical his face was, and I was damn sure his tongue was pierced.

"Who did you say your grandmother was? I probably know her. Havenwood Falls is that kind of town."

Swell. The corner of my lips curved. "I didn't say."

He shifted the car in neutral, and taking the keys with him, stepped out of the car. His full height, which I guessed to be just over six feet, forced me to tip my head back to look him in the eyes. Something about the violet color intrigued me, a glint in the irises that wasn't normal. He arched a brow as he waited for a name.

I had prolonged intentionally. "Layla Whitt."

"Seriously?"

My eyes narrowed. "What is that supposed to mean?"

"Nothing. I just didn't know she had a granddaughter."

He wasn't telling me something, and I wanted to press him. I didn't like secrets, and it had become clear that he was hiding something. "Yeah, well, this is my first time in Havenwood Falls. Actually, in Colorado."

"So you're a . . ." He left the unfinished question dangling as if he was second-guessing himself. Those unusual eyes bored into mine.

"I'm what?" I prompted, watching as he grabbed the hooky-thingamabob from the back of his truck.

He glanced over his shoulder while he secured the anchor under my car, and I caught the flash of a tattoo on his forearm. The movement had been too quick for me to get a clear view, but I was intrigued.

"A sophomore?" he posed.

That was so not what was on his mind. *What gives?* Torent Stark was hiding something, but why? What could he possibly know about me or my family? "No, I'm a senior."

Straightening up, he dusted off his hands on his jeans. "That's got to be rough, changing schools in the middle of a semester."

The sun was at his back, highlighting the sides of his cheekbones. Of all the people to meet first in Havenwood Falls, I had to encounter the most roguish of guys.

I shrugged. When hadn't my life been rough? "It's only seven months. I'll manage."

Something glittered in his eyes. "So you don't plan on sticking around after?"

Were all the people here this talkative? "Just long enough to graduate, and then I'm off to college."

Sauntering back to the truck, he wrenched open the door. "Havenwood Falls might surprise you. Who knows, you might find a reason to stick around." The lopsided smirk he aimed at me made my stomach cartwheel.

Was he implying *he* might be worth sticking around for? How presumptuous. I didn't even know him and wasn't positive I wanted to, regardless of how he made my insides react.

With that carnal grin still playing on his lips, Torent jumped into the truck to hit the button. In under a minute, my car was safely out of the ditch and back on the road. There might have been one or two scratches to commemorate my first day in Havenwood Falls, but I was more concerned about the mark Torent Stark had left on me.

"How much do I owe you?" I asked, tilting my head to the side as he slid out of the truck to lean against the side.

"It's on the house. Consider it a welcoming gift." A breeze blew through from the surrounding mountains, picking up pieces of his wind-tousled hair and sweeping them over one eye.

The urge to reach up and brush the loose strand of hair rose up inside me. I hadn't expected it.

"You really don't have to do that," I insisted, shoving my hands in my pockets before I did something stupid—like touched him.

"I know. But maybe you'll remember what a nice guy I was once you start school."

I gave him a funny look. "Are you saying you're not a nice guy?"

His gaze dropped and ran over my face. Something was there I couldn't quite grasp—a warning? "Definitely not. Welcome to Havenwood Falls, crash car. See you Monday." He dropped the keys into my hand.

Not if I can help it.

Slipping into the driver's seat, I put the keys into the ignition and turned. The car cranked over once before finally starting.

"Thanks for your help," I said, looking up at him with a straight face, the door still open.

He winked. "Anytime."

I didn't plan on making a habit of being rescued by Torent Stark. Something told me to stay far and clear from him. I sat in my car, frowning as Stark got into the truck. I knew guys like him. They were distractions, the kind that got you pregnant before graduation, and that was the very last thing I wanted.

To be my mom.

CHAPTER 2

J pulled into the long driveway lined with aspen trees. The gold and orange leaves made the trees seem as if they were on fire. Fall was in full bloom, colors popping in the flowerbed surrounding the large porch of Gigi's house.

As I opened the car door, the smell of burning wood blew in with the crisp breeze that rattled the leaves overhead. I huddled deeper into my Wisconsin Badger hoodie.

Gigi's house was nestled deep in Havenwood Falls, outside of town. I'd always looked forward to Gigi's visits. Eccentric she was, but it was one of the many things I adored about her. I knew very little about the town where Gigi lived. Odd, considering Mom grew up here, but she didn't like to talk about her past.

Coming home to live with Gigi was a slap in the face, and it took every ounce of willpower Mom had to come back here and ask for help. Pride had made her stay away for seventeen years.

And it only took three failed marriages for her to return home.

Grabbing a box from the backseat, I hiked it up the porch. Gigi and Mom were waiting for me, having heard my car pull up.

"You made it, sunshine." Gigi placed her soft hands on my cheeks, and followed with a kiss. Her silvery hair still shone with highlights of her former color, honey blond like mine. It was long and wavy, framing her oval face. Gigi wasn't like most grandmothers, and it wasn't just that she looked fabulous for her age, with only the lightest of wrinkles crinkling at the corners of her eyes. Her mind was sharp, her tongue was loose, and she had an aura of energy about her.

I adored the ever-loving crap out of her. Unlike Mom, I was ecstatic to see her. Handing the box over to Mom, I gave Gigi a proper hug. "It was no big deal. The guy at the garage pulled out my car, and there was no permanent damage."

"Joshua?" she asked.

I shook my head. "No, his name was Torent."

Gigi's lips twitched, a twinkling moving into her aqua eyes. "Ah, the Stark boy. He's your age, if I recall. The youngest of the three boys."

"He mentioned he had two brothers."

That gleam in her eyes intensified. "Did he now?"

Oh no. I knew that look. It was the one she got when she was plotting something. "Don't start. I'm only here until I graduate, and the last thing I need is you trying to set me up with a guy."

"I agree," Mom added, in case we wanted her opinion. She shifted the box to her hip. The last beams of sun caught the side of her face, picking up the platinum blond streaks she added to her hair. "Mallory is smart. She's going places, going to be someone." Everything Mom had always wanted, when she had put aside her dreams to have me.

"Are you still aiming for that swimming scholarship?" Gigi asked.

I nodded. "If I can keep up my grades, then I have a chance. My coach promised to write a letter of recommendation on my behalf."

"You'll get that scholarship. No one deserves it more than you," Gigi boasted, my personal cheerleader.

"Thanks." I smiled, needing that little boost of confidence.

She draped an arm around my waist. "Let's get you settled in. I've got your mom's old room ready for you."

"Wonderful," Mom said, rolling her eyes.

"Don't worry, Wendy. I had the loft on the third floor made up for you. Lots of privacy." Gigi winked at me.

This would be an interesting year.

~

STANDING in front of my car, I stared at the three-story red brick building, watching as the hordes of teens rushed into the school through the arched doorways. I took a deep breath. For a flicker of a moment, I contemplated hopping back into my car and driving up into the mountains, away from all my doubts and insecurities. But then I reminded myself: ten months—that was all I had until I got the piece of paper that would allow me to pursue my dreams. I wasn't going to give up on my swimming.

Here goes nothing.

I moved with the crowds, blending in as I made my way to the front office of Havenwood Falls High. It wasn't hard to find. Principal Friske's name was on the door. I gave the woman behind the desk my name, and she handed me a printout of my schedule and locker number with the combination. The basics. Every school had them.

"Books will be handed out in the classrooms," the secretary informed me.

I nodded and took the slip of paper, giving it a once-over. AP Statistics. French III. Physics. AP Lit. Lunch. Blah. Blah. Blah. It was all very similar to my classes in my old school.

Locker number 256.

HFH wasn't difficult to navigate. As I walked down the halls, the upcoming homecoming dance seemed to be a hot topic. I passed a group of rowdy football players chanting "Kase Kasun," who I assumed was a key player.

I found my locker easily. It was the combinations that were always tricky. By the third unsuccessful try, I was about to kick the darn thing when I heard a familiar voice.

"Hey, crash car."

I dropped my forehead onto the locker. *Why?* I asked myself as a swarm of glowing fireflies fluttered in my belly. A body leaned on the gray locker beside mine, and I turned my head to the side to stare at Torent Stark.

Damn.

Why couldn't he have been less attractive than I remembered?

An easy smile crossed his full lips, and the conversation in the hall faded as I gazed into his eyes. They were as bright and mischievous as before. Several of the girls walking by glanced over their shoulders to stare, and who could blame them? Torent had this rock star quality that grabbed everyone's attention, including mine, and I didn't like it.

His jeans hung low on his hips, so when he lifted his hand to run his fingers through his already tousled hair, his black T-shirt tightened against his chest. Torent Stark reeked of danger. I could hear my best friend from Wisconsin, Addison, in my head telling me I needed a dose of danger, that my life was too safe, too boring.

She might be right, but that didn't mean I would fall for the charms of a guy like Torent.

I needed to stop gawking at him and say something that wouldn't sound lame. "Hey."

Yep. Not lame at all.

He plucked the slip of paper from my fingers. "Let's see." His eyes scanned down my schedule. "Wow, crash car. You've got brains."

"Does that intimidate you?" I challenged, lifting my brows. Was I flirting? *Stop it. No flirting allowed.*

A lazy grin curved up one side of his lips. "Nah. I dig brains."

Wonderful.

"Do you need help with that?" he asked, nodding his head at the finicky locker.

"It's all yours," I said, stepping aside to give him a crack. How had I not noticed the little scar on his right eyebrow the other day? It only added to his rebel without a cause persona.

The locker clicked open, pulling my gaze away from his face. "Voilà. It just takes a magic touch."

And I bet Torent had fingers of magic. "Thanks."

"It looks like we have first period together. I'll walk you to class."

"How gallant of you." I shoved a stack of binders and notebooks inside the locker, keeping one of each in my hands before slamming the door shut.

"The car okay?" His lips twitched at the reminder of our first encounter.

My eyes were drawn to his mouth before I forced them to meet his gaze. "For now. I'm surprised it made the trip all the way from Wisconsin," I admitted.

A pretty raven-haired girl sauntered up behind Torent, looping her arms around his waist and resting her chin on his shoulder.

"Who's your new friend?" she asked with a sneer, dark blue eyes assessing me. She made her intentions very clear. Torent Stark was hers.

He has a girlfriend. That was what ran through my head, along with an irrational amount of disappointment. Of course he had a girlfriend. Just look at the guy.

Unless I was mistaken, Torent wasn't pleased with the interruption. The muscle along his jaw tightened. "Mallory Dorian, this is Brooklyn Kendall."

"Pleasure," Brooklyn replied in a condescending tone and quickly dismissed me, returning her attention to Torent. "I missed you last night," she murmured in his ear.

I thought I caught a flicker of annoyance in his eyes, as he unraveled Brooklyn's arms from around his waist. "I had to work."

She huffed, her Cupid's bow mouth turning down into a pretty pout. Brooklyn looked like the girl who was used to getting what she wanted. "Remind me why again? It's not like you need the money."

I felt like an intruder listening in on the conversation, and awkwardness followed.

Buzzzzzzzzzzzz.

Thank God. Saved by the bell. The first period warning sounded through the halls, giving us five minutes to get to class. I thought about just slipping into the stream of kids moving down the hall, doubting Torent or Brooklyn would notice I was gone.

"You know why," Torent replied, letting a teensy bit of exasperation leak into his voice. "Mallory and I have first period together. I'll see you later."

Brooklyn wasn't going to be brushed off so easily. She twisted her midnight hair around her finger and laid her other hand on Torent's arm. "I'm sure she can get to homeroom without a babysitter. It's not like Havenwood Falls High is a labyrinth."

I was positive I had just made my first enemy, and it only took what, ten minutes? Boom. New record. Girls like her ruined the high school experience. "Seriously, it's fine. I need to learn my way around on my own. I can't have you walking me to every class."

Brooklyn's blue eyes darkened, and not giving Torent a chance to overrule me, I turned and melded into the crowd, but not before I caught a glimpse of the scowl on his perfect lips.

Ugh.

Get him out of your brain, Mal. He's not for you.

I SURVIVED the first half of the day with only a dash of humiliation. It could have been worse. And I had only gotten lost twice, but the day wasn't over yet.

The cafeteria was no different than my last high school. Grease coated the air, along with subtle hints of perfume, sweat, and teenage angst. Between the scents and my nerves, I could kiss my appetite goodbye.

A guy with shaggy blue hair sighed and plopped down next to me at the empty lunch table. "God, what I wouldn't do for just five minutes alone in the janitor's closet with that."

I hadn't realized I'd been staring until the newcomer caught me. His gaze, like mine, was fixed on Torent and Brooklyn strolling into the cafeteria as if they owned the place, looking like the perfect high school couple.

"She is pretty," I admitted, never mind that the admission felt like sandpaper in my throat.

He made a face, scrunching his nose. "Honey, I wasn't talking about the she-devil. Brooklyn Kendall is as ugly inside as she is out."

I think I just found my new BFF. My expression must have still held disappointment at seeing how cozy Brooklyn was with Torent.

"Uh-oh. Don't tell me the infamous Torent has already claimed another victim? The guy has been breaking hearts since kindergarten."

I stiffened my shoulders and forced my eyes back to my veggie wrap, reminding myself why I was here. "Definitely not."

"That's what we all say," he said, flashing me an award-winning grin. "Beck Winslow."

I smiled in return. "Mallory Dorian."

His gray eyes twinkled, matching the silver hoop in his eyebrow. "I know who you are. Everyone does."

"Fabulous," I groaned. Torent and Brooklyn had joined a group on the other side of the room, sitting down.

Beck's gaze followed mine. "He does have a very fine ass. If he even thinks about jumping to the other team, I'm throwing myself at him."

I laughed, unable to help myself. Something about Beck and the way he said whatever crazy thing on his mind reminded me of Addison. She would have loved him, blue hair, black earplugs, a touch of nerd, and all.

He lifted a brow. "You think I'm joking."

"Does it matter?" I retorted, picking at my sandwich.

"I knew I would like you." Just as Torent had done, Beck plucked my schedule from atop my notebook, which had been sitting on the table. His eyes read down the column. "Girl's got brains. Thank God you're not another boy-crazed bimbo with big boobs."

"Nope. No big boobs here," I pointed out.

Plucking an apple from his food tray, he grinned. "With that face, who needs them?"

I smiled. It was nice to have a friend, someone I could relate to, and I had a really good feeling about Beck.

He took a bite out of the shiny red apple, eyes returning to scroll down my schedule. "It looks like we're going to be study buddies. Not counting lunch, we have four classes together, including first period with the heart-stealing Torent, I might add."

I groaned. I hadn't noticed Beck during first period, but that was probably because I couldn't take my eyes off Torent. He was definitely not going to be good for my GPA, but as luck would have it, so far, it was the only class we had together.

Beck handed me back my schedule, meeting my gaze head on. "Don't let Brooklyn get to you. Pretty girls threaten her, and by the ferocious scowl she's aiming at your back, she knows she's got competition."

"Good to know. So should I come to school tomorrow looking like a hag to get off her radar?"

Something colorful about Beck delighted me. I couldn't place my finger on it, but it wasn't just his hair color. "On anyone else, that might work, but you've already caught the attention of what she considers hers. HFH's cutie."

Goodie gumdrops. I didn't have to ask who he was talking about. "What's their deal? Is she his girlfriend?" I couldn't believe I was even asking. What did I care if he had a girlfriend?

I don't care.

Yep. It wasn't working.

"What day is it?" he asked, looking thoughtful.

I wrinkled my nose.

He was quick to fill me in on the HFH gossip. "Those two are on again, off again. It's dizzying. Who knows, maybe they're back on, but last I heard through the Havenwood Falls gossip chain, Torent had broken things off."

I nibbled on my lower lip. Interesting.

No! There is nothing interesting about Torent.

Beck leaned down on the table, lowering his voice. "Just be careful with Brooklyn. She isn't afraid to get dirty, and being a Whitt puts a target on your back even without lusting after Torent."

"I'm not lusting after him," I defended myself, but it sounded weak, even to me. Then it dawned on me that he had referred to Gigi. "Why does my family have anything to do with Brooklyn's dislike of me?"

Now it was his turn to give me an odd sideways glance. His hand reached along the table and grabbed both my arms, flipping them over.

"No hidden tattoos?" he asked, eyes searching over my body.

Okay, this just got weird.

"Should I?" Did I look like a girl who got her body inked?

Releasing both my arms, he leaned back in the plastic chair, observing me with open curiosity. What was I missing here?

"Interesting," he mumbled to himself, his fingers brushing over his chin.

"I'm going to need more than that. What is interesting? Are tattoos like a prerequisite here or something?" I was joking, but a flicker in Beck's face gave me pause.

He laughed in an awkward cover-up kind of way. "No, of course not."

Nice try. What was he hiding? What did tattoos have to do with it? Now that my mind was on alert, I remembered that Torent had a tattoo. And so did Beck. I had caught a quick glimpse of it on the back of his neck, just above the shirt collar.

"You have a tattoo," I pointed out.

His hand moved to rub at the top of his spine. "Yeah, a drunk night regret. I don't recommend it. Puking after having a needle repeatedly stabbed into your neck? Not a fun time."

"Noted," I said, taking a sip of my water, but I wasn't buying the whole I-got-drunk-and-woke-up-with-a-tattoo routine.

And as I went about the rest of the day, I noticed more and more students had them. On their arms, wrists, ankles. I was positive even Brooklyn herself had one. That star-shaped beauty mark above her lip —it was too seamless to be DNA.

For the most part, Havenwood Falls High was like any other school I'd been to. I didn't know why that surprised me. There were the usual cliques, the muscle-bound jocks, the math nerds, the dark artsy group, the all-too-perfect plastics, the dramatic theater kids, and everyone else in between.

And then me.

The shiny new girl—who everyone stared at like I was a sparkling Christmas bauble. I hated the attention.

The bell rang.
It was finally the best part of the day—the end.

CHAPTER 3

$\mathcal{A}$fter school, I only wanted one thing—to relax and unwind. Sitting in my car, I flipped the little key card to the Creekwood Country Club in my hand.

"Why the hell not?" I said out loud.

If there was a pool within my reach, I would be in it, and the prospect of a steaming sauna afterward was too much to resist. I stuck the keys into my car and let the engine rip to life—or in my car's case, sputter.

I would have to take it sooner than later for its own sort of pampering, which had nothing to do with a certain part-time mechanic/tow truck driver.

I loved when I fooled myself.

The Creekwood Country Club had all the amenities you would expect—golfing, ski access, a nice restaurant, a full-service spa, and a private lounge with a bar. But it had only one amenity that I cared about—two, if you counted the sauna.

A lap pool was inside a glass enclosure with breathtaking views every which way you looked. It connected to the outside smaller pleasure pool and Jacuzzi. Due to the briskness in the air, I chose to stay inside.

Quickly changing in the lockers, I dropped a towel and my cell phone onto an empty lounge chair. I had the pool to myself, and my excitement went up a notch. It was too early for the older crowd still pushing the nine-to-five, and I seriously doubted the country club was considered a hotspot for the local teens to hang out.

Which made it my perfect sanctuary.

I'd swum varsity since my freshman year, and during the summers, I had worked at the local YMCA giving lessons. It was hard knowing I wouldn't be competing this year, but it didn't mean I had to give it up completely.

As I stared at the calm, crystal-blue water, all I wanted to do was get my butt in the pool and lose myself. I swore, sometimes it seemed as if the water whispered my name, enchanting me.

I slid into the pool and sighed, letting the balmy temperature rush over my skin. There were eight lanes in the lap pool, and I waded over to one in the middle. Warming up with some freestyle laps, I transitioned into the backstroke.

I loved swimming, the feel of the cool water rushing over my face as I glided effortlessly with the waves. It called to me, like a song, and I was powerless to do anything but answer. And then there was the mesmerizing light as it played and changed the deeper I dived.

I'd been swimming my whole life. It was a part of me as much as breathing was, and even when my lungs begged for air, I pushed myself, swimming on through the smooth blue water, strong and sure. Beads of water stuck to my eyelashes as I emerged through the surface, letting the sun warm my golden skin through the glass enclosure, and stared into Torent's stormy eyes.

A little squeak escaped at finding I was no longer alone.

"You scared me," I exhaled, using that as an excuse for the sudden spike in my heart rate.

"So you swim?" he asked, crouching down to the edge of the pool. He was fully clothed in the same black jeans, but had changed his shirt. It was identical to the one he had worn the day we met, Havenwood Falls Garage & Tow Service embroidered into the left breast. I had no clue how, but he managed to make the plain T-shirt sexy.

"There's a lot of things I do. Swimming is just one of them," I replied coolly, feeling pretty smug. I was not going to make a fool of myself around some guy. That's all he was—just a random guy. No one special.

Curiosity spread over his expression as he stared at me with an intense gaze. "You're different than the other girls."

I rested my arms on the edge of the concrete, the tips of my toes barely touching the bottom. "Because I swim?"

One side of his lips curved into a lopsided smirk. "I'm not sure yet. I can't place my finger on it, but there is something about you I find unique."

I could say the same thing about him, but in my case, I had a reasonable explanation. "It's because I'm the new girl."

We studied each other for a deep moment, neither of us moving. Hell, I barely blinked; I was so entranced by the color of his eyes.

He let his fingers dip into the water, nearly brushing my arm. "Maybe, but I don't think that's it."

"Are you always this forward?"

His expression turned impish as he flashed me a pair of killer dimples. "Usually. I'm used to getting what I want."

Was he implying that he wanted me? Well, too bad. I wasn't a possession he could acquire because he got an inkling. I was here to get my diploma and get on to the life I wanted to live. "What are you doing at the club? Stalking me?"

"Just making a drop-off. The shop did some repairs on a golf cart."

"Oh." My eyes glanced over his head to the clock on the wall. I needed to get home. Lifting up on my arms, I climbed out of the pool to see Torent standing and swinging my towel on his finger.

"Hand it over," I said, giving him a dry look.

His eyes swept over me in a slow perusal that did funny things to my belly—warm, gooey things. "Nice set."

And then he opened his mouth and said that. Typical pig. I lifted my brows.

"The swimsuit," he added, grinning like a total shithead.

Oh, he thought he was so witty.

"I'm sure that's what you meant." *Dickhead.* "Shouldn't you be working or rubbing your girlfriend's feet instead of bothering me?" *And ruining the only quiet I've had all day.*

His brow shot up. "You're referring to Brooklyn, I assume."

I wrapped the towel under my arms and tucked the corner in above my chest.

"You have more than one girlfriend. Go figure," I mumbled under my breath.

"I don't . . . have a girlfriend," he added.

I shrugged, dripping water on the concrete floor. "It really doesn't matter to me." *Lies!*

He moved closer and leaned into my space. "Then why bring it up?"

I wanted to duck under the nearest lounge chair and hit my head on the ground. Why indeed had I? Heat gathered in my cheeks, his nearness causing a shiver to roll through me. "I just don't want any crazy jealous girlfriend slashing my tires at school."

Amusing him wasn't what I had in mind, but his lips twitched, and I swore a glint of gold flecks sparkled in his violet eyes. "Brooklyn does have a tendency to overreact, but she isn't mentally unstable."

I took a step back and gathered the rest of my things. "I'll take your word for it. I need to get home."

"Goodbye, Mal." The husky way he shortened my name made my heart sigh, regardless of the fact that I didn't want to feel anything in his presence.

I padded into the shower room, not bothering to shower. I just changed and raced out of the locker room, eager to get home without any other run-ins with he who must not be named. Unfortunately, I bumped into someone way worse.

Brooklyn Kendall and two of her faithful followers.

Someone shoot me now. I wasn't up to having a faceoff with Havenwood Falls' queen bee.

Brooklyn was standing just outside the pool entrance with two other girls, staring at me like the Wicked Witch of the West. Her long glossy midnight hair was pulled back into a ponytail, and her sapphire eyes glared with gobs of hatred.

"Oh, hey." Internally, I cringed. The sight of Brooklyn at the club destroyed its perfect little haven appeal. I had really been hoping for a spot in Havenwood Falls I could call my own, feel comfortable. A pool might not be the right place.

She folded her arms, popping her curvy hip out to one side. "Ladies, let me make introductions. This is Mallory, you know, the new girl."

I stiffened. Would everything out of Brooklyn's mouth always be so snooty?

"Mallory, this is Leena Avon and Cora Sheldon. My squad."

Bitch squad was what she actually meant. The two girls were as flawless as Brooklyn—no shocker—with stunning faces and well put together outfits you only saw in magazines.

Then there was me. Wet hair. T-shirt with damp spots. Ripped jeans. And my favorite worn out Converse. In comparison, I felt poor and frumpy. Brooklyn and me, we weren't even in the same category.

"Nice to meet you," I replied with a smile, doing my best to be nice.

"Wow. That was an impressive backstroke." Leena flipped her dark hair over one shoulder. She was striking, slim, tall, and her skin was a beautiful sun-dusted color of bronze.

"I'll say. A little too good. No one can swim those times without some extra help," Brooklyn sneered.

Was she suggesting I was on drugs? "I don't know what you mean. I used to compete back in Wisconsin. I was the captain of my swim team."

"Cute," Brooklyn replied as if my life story was the most boring thing in the world, next to watching her dog get a bath.

"Do you guys swim?" I asked, attempting to make small talk, seeing as they made no indication of letting me walk past.

Cora shook her bubble-gum pink hair. She reminded me of a Strawberry Shortcake doll. "Not competitively. We just like to hang out at the club."

Brooklyn jabbed her in the side, as if Cora had said something she shouldn't. "I know you're new here and all. Let me give you a friendly bit of advice."

Ha. Friendly my ass. Here it comes. The real reason she stopped me.

The fake smile disappeared from her lips. "It's probably best if you stayed away from Torent Stark. I wouldn't want you to tarnish your family's name. Isn't that right, ladies?"

Cora and Leena nodded eagerly, but I seriously doubted either of them had a single thought for themselves. It was obvious they got all of their direction from Brooklyn, probably even how much sugar to put in their coffee, like little obedient robots.

"What are you talking about?" I prodded. I wanted Brooklyn to know she couldn't intimidate me.

A chilly look entered her eyes. "You haven't lived here as long as we have. The Stark family has a bad reputation—criminals, scoundrels, the usual bad apples."

"But didn't you date him?" I countered, wondering why she would pursue him so hard if he had such a nasty reputation.

"Right, making him off limits." She puckered her glossy lips.

Okay, that didn't make any sense, but I wasn't going to stand here damp, arguing her logic. I also wouldn't let her bully me. Who the hell did she think she was, telling me who I should and shouldn't talk to? Please. I wasn't a member of her *squad* she could order about.

"Thanks for the warning, but I think I can judge for myself who's not worth my time." And Brooklyn was at the top of the list.

I brushed past the bitch squad, leaving all three of them gaping after me. The shock on their faces brought a smile to my lips, but I knew I would pay for it. Regardless of what Torent thought of Brooklyn's character, I didn't trust her. She smacked of revenge.

CHAPTER 4

Tomorrow was Friday, and that meant I had nearly survived a week at HFH. How hard could the rest of the year be?

Skipping off the sidewalk into the parking lot, I searched for my car, remembering I had parked in the back lot today. Timing was everything when it came to getting a premium spot, as I found out this morning when I'd been running late.

My mind was a million miles away, thinking about school, Addison, and what parties she would attend without me, and I didn't notice the weird angle my car sat at until I was in front of it.

"You've got to be freaking kidding." I stared at my lopsided car and massaged the side of my temple, feeling the headache I'd been fighting all day roar to life. The tire on the driver's side was flatter than my Mom's pancakes. "Son of a bitch," I hissed, sinking against the car.

Of course, I didn't have a spare. Why would I?

I had taken it out to make more room in my trunk for the move. *Smart move, Mallory. I bet you're really regretting that now.*

A chorus of giggles from across the lot caught my attention. Who else would it be but Brooklyn, Cora, and Leena, the three wicked witches. Steam blew out of my ears as my hands clenched together. I was about to go storming over there and grab Brooklyn by her ponytail when I heard a deep voice.

"Hey, crash car, looks like you've got a bit of a problem."

I groaned. Of all the people in the school, Torent Stark was the last person I wanted to see or ask for help.

"I'm going to pop your girlfriend's implants," I growled.

His gaze followed my glaring eye line. "Brooklyn? I told you she isn't my—"

"Save it," I interrupted. "I'm not in the mood for another 'we're just friends' lecture."

"Who spit in your latte?"

"Do you really have to ask?"

He ran a hand through his dark hair.

"I'll take care of her," he said in a short voice that sent a tremor down my spine.

I pulled my glare from Brooklyn to look at Torent. Those gold specks were back. "I'm not sure anyone can control the hurricane known as Brooklyn Kendall."

He leaned one hand on the open car door and the other on the roof, keeping me boxed against the car with his body. "No truer words might have been spoken. But seriously, she'll listen to me."

I ignored the warm fuzzies inside my belly. "It couldn't hurt. But I'm warning you, if she doesn't back down, things are going to get ugly."

"I might just put my money on you." He nodded over his shoulder. "Come on. I'll give you a lift home."

Chewing on my lip, I wondered if it was a good idea for me to be alone in a confined space with him. "What about my car? I can't leave it here."

He had an answer for everything. "I'll come back and take it to the shop, fix the tire, and have it dropped off tonight."

Damn. Why was he being so nice? It was making it really hard to hate him. "You don't have to do that. I can call the garage."

He pushed his hands into his back pockets and rocked on his heels. "And you would still get me."

Right. How could I forget? "Fine. I'd thank you, but I don't want it to go to your head."

"Smart," he agreed, grinning.

"At least you got that right." I grabbed my bag and dropped my car keys into his open palm once again.

Following him to his black Jeep, he surprised me by opening the passenger door for me. Our fingers accidentally brushed as I hopped to get inside. Tiny sparks of electricity ignited on contact.

"Ouch. You shocked me," I accused, sitting in the bucket seat.

"We're electric," he replied with a wicked grin.

A frown pulled at my lips.

"That's totally what I was thinking," I retorted dryly.

He shut the car door, and I watched him go around to the driver's side. My lips formed a tight line as I repeatedly told myself there was nothing special about this guy, that he didn't look every bit as delicious as I imagined.

The engine purred to life, and my gaze dropped to his lips. For each butterfly flutter I felt in my belly, my irritation mounted. So what if his car smelled amazing and I wanted to roll around in it? So what if he made my pulse race whenever he was near?

"This is all your fault," I hurled at him after a few minutes of stewing. We were at the end of the school driveway, getting ready to pull out onto First Street.

"How so?"

I stared straight ahead, watching the road roll by. "Your girlfriend thinks you're flirting with me."

"I am," he said, causing my head to whip toward him. He was grinning. "And she's not my girlfriend."

"Tell that to her," I mumbled, sinking further into the seat.

His fingers held the steering wheel loosely, like he was born to drive. "Oh, trust me, Brooklyn and I are going to have a talk. She has issues with boundaries."

"I'll say," I grumbled. "She cornered me at the club and basically told me she owned you."

That brought a dark scowl to his face.

"No one owns me," he stated with a serious intensity.

I shifted uncomfortably in the seat. For the first time, I could see the danger that lay buried inside Torent. Brooklyn hadn't been kidding about him being dangerous. "Why do I get the feeling there is more to this thing between Brooklyn and me?"

He gave me a slow grin that had my breath catching. "Maybe because you have stellar intuition."

"Are you going to tell me or make me beg?"

"Begging sounds good."

I hit him playfully on the shoulder. "Never going to happen."

He was somehow overwhelmingly close. "Never say never, Mal. I bet I could make you beg."

Holy crap. Was it getting hot in here? Time to stick to the topic, and no more sexual innuendoes in a closed car with Torent. He was too tempting.

"Can you think about something other than sex?"

"I'm a guy. What do you expect?"

"Tell me what you know," I demanded.

He sighed, swinging his truck into the wooded driveway. "I don't know details, only that something happened between her family and yours back in the day. Some kind of beef."

"Beef?" I echoed, staring at the cozy cottage that was now my home. "Gigi is the sweetest woman on the planet. What could possibly cause tension between our families?"

He shrugged, letting the car roll to a stop. "I told you. I don't have details. Brooklyn and I didn't spend a lot of time discussing her family."

Great. Now I had images of him doing *things* with Brooklyn, and it induced an unreasonable bout of jealousy inside me. It was a good thing we were already at Gigi's, or I might have jumped from his moving Jeep. I pulled the door handle.

"I just bet you didn't." Then I hopped out and slammed the door, hoping it would make me feel better. It didn't.

As I started to stomp across the lawn, Torent's laugh reached me, fueling a fresh fit of rage. I gave him the one figure salute. *Take that, Torent Stark.*

His damn roguish laugh only grew louder.

Gah. For good measure, I lifted my other hand in the air, mimicking the gesture.

Behind me, the crunching tires of his truck slowly backed out of the driveway, and I hiked up the porch.

"How was your day?" Gigi asked from the swing. A hint of a smile played on her lips.

I dropped my bag near the front door and slumped down beside her. The wood creaked and swayed under my weight. "Utter shit."

Gigi didn't bat an eye at my language. She was used to much worse from my mother, so I doubted anything I could do or say would surprise her. "Is that why you were giving the Stark boy such a rude finger gesture?"

"Yes, it was." Why did I let Torent get under my skin? I wrinkled my nose. "It was nothing he didn't deserve."

The swing glided smoothly underneath us. "Do you want to talk about it?"

I snorted. "Not in this century."

"DINNER!" Gigi called from downstairs.

Thank God. A distraction I could get behind. Food.

And not Mom's.

Sitting in my room, pretending to do homework, was not going well. Especially when I couldn't get Torent's face out of my head. Those damn dimples.

Dinner at the Whitts' residence was a bit tense. For as long as I could remember, Gigi and Mom never saw eye-to-eye regarding anything.

"So how did the job hunt go, Wendy?" Gigi asked Mom as she passed the salad bowl.

"Are you going to hound me every night?" Mom snapped back.

"I got an A on my Chemistry test today," I quickly interjected, trying to defuse the situation before it spun out of control.

"So you're adjusting well to school then?" Gigi asked, slicing a piece of beef she had roasted in the crockpot.

I shrugged, pushing the salad around on my plate.

"For the most part." I did my best to keep any distress from leaking into my voice.

Gigi picked up on it regardless. Sometimes I thought she had psychic abilities. She had an eerie way of sensing emotions. "Does it have anything to do with the boy?"

"What boy?" Mom asked, perking up at the mention of a guy. Just like Mom. Some things never changed.

"No. Definitely not." *Liar!* my mind screamed.

Mom grinned, lifting her fork to her mouth. "Then why are your cheeks suddenly red?"

Mom was a quandary. One minute she was all, "Stay away from boys, Mallory," and the next, she was picking out which hot guy should be my prom date.

"Because it's hot in here." What a sad excuse. No one would believe that.

"Who is this boy who doesn't have you all worked up?" Mom asked, stabbing a forkful of greens.

"Torent Stark," Gigi answered for me.

"Gigi," I hissed, ready to drop my face into my plate of mashed potatoes.

"Seriously?" Mom asked, raising her brows. "Wow."

I frowned at her from across the table. "Why is that such a surprise? You know his family?"

"Yeah. I went to school with his mom, Raina. I wouldn't have pegged him as your type. He's a little rough around the edges, don't you think?"

"Didn't you know his father as well?" Gigi added.

Mom stared at her plate, looking a bit lost in the past for a moment. "Calmar Stark." I swore she shuddered when she said his name, and the tightening of her mouth wasn't a mirage. "He went to the Academy."

I assumed she meant the private school here in Havenwood Falls. I didn't know much about it, other than I'd overheard Willa Kasun say something about Sun and Moon Academy during lunch the other day.

"Why do I get the feeling you don't like his father?" I questioned.

Her expression turned serious, and it unnerved me. "Just do me a favor. Be careful."

Mom had a reason for running away from this place and never looking back until now. More than ever, I wanted to unearth why. What happened seventeen years ago? I'd always thought it was because of something between Mom, Gigi, and my father, but now I wasn't so sure.

"What exactly should I be worried about?"

Mom waved her fork at me. "Just who you pick as your friends. I don't want you getting mixed up with the wrong crowds."

And just who constituted as the wrong crowd?

"Like Brooklyn Kendall?" I asked, testing the reaction of the table.

Dead silence.

No one moved a single muscle.

Wow. That wasn't exactly what I envisioned happening, and now my curiosity about the past exploded to new levels.

Gigi and Mom shared a look. For once, it looked like they might be in agreement on something. Keeping me in the dark.

"Is that what happened to your tire today at school?" Mom concluded.

Crap. I hadn't meant for this to be turned back around on me. "I'm sure I just ran over a nail. Flat tires happen all the time."

"Not in Havenwood Falls," Mom mumbled under her breath.

What did that mean?

CHAPTER 5

*H*ello, weekend.

It was Saturday, and I had no homework, no plans, and nothing to do, but I wasn't going to waste the day binge-watching reruns of *Vampire Diaries*. Besides, Gigi's TV reception sucked. What was with this place and technology? It was as if it was so far off the grid, nothing worked.

As promised, Torent had my car returned by the next morning, looking good as new. So instead of being cooped up all day, I was going to explore.

It was a beautiful, sunny fall day, one of the few left in October. The air was the perfect sweater weather temperature, and I'd been dying to check out the falls.

Tugging on a soft blue hoodie, I secured my blond hair into a messy bun and tied the laces on my Converse. I tucked my cell phone into my pocket and trotted down the stairs into the kitchen, grabbing a bottle of water and my car keys off the counter.

"I'm going out!" I yelled through the house, hoping someone heard me.

The drive to the falls wasn't far from where Gigi lived. I continued down Blackstone Road, and a tingle danced up my arms, causing my thoughts to travel back to the dinner conversation the other night. I made a mental note to grill Beck on any gossip he might have heard about my family.

I needed answers.

A cemetery sat to the right, and I whipped my car to the side of the road. Not creepy at all. Locking my car up, I hiked across the street. The falls, according to the map, should have been straight ahead through the woods from the cemetery. I didn't claim to be a great outdoorsman, but how hard could it be to find?

After an hour of wandering around in the woods, I knew one thing—I was lost.

"Shit," I swore. No question about it. One glimpse at my cell phone told me I was in deep crap. No service. Of course not.

I'd never been amazing at directions. *Thank you, Mom.* I must have somehow ended up walking too far to the west.

Turning around in circles, I stared through the blue spruces and towering cottonwoods. It all looked the same. I was about to panic when I picked up the sound of running water. I rushed toward the crashing of water, and when the woods finally gave way to a clearing, my entire body sighed.

Water rushed over low cliffs in a trio of falls dropping into a sparkling crystal pool of blue-green that looked like glass. I stood at the edge, breathing in the air flowing around me.

It wasn't as large as I had pictured, not by any means, but that didn't mean it was any less spectacular. The colors and textures of the water and the angle of the light intrigued me.

Mallory.

The water whispered my name. It wasn't an unusual thing. I'd been hearing the call of the lake my whole life, but something unique about the pool of the falls gave me pause.

I saw a flash, a glint shimmering like gold in the sunlight carving through the water, and for an instant, a spark of blue swirled like fairy dust, then was gone.

What was that?

Slipping out of my shoes, I waded into the shallow edge of the lake, dirt and sand squishing between my toes. I gasped at the bite of coldness, but after a moment, it didn't bother me.

Strange.

Most people would think me insane to go into the water at this time of year, but I couldn't explain it. I was compelled.

I let my fingers skim over the surface, feeling the water. An uninterested silver fish swam past me, on his way to the falls, where the water was bubbling. I stepped farther in, the water coming up past my knees, and a gentle hum filled the air. It was as if the lake was saying, *Welcome home, Mallory. What's taken you so long? We've been waiting.*

I blinked, feeling slightly disoriented, but I shook it off, going deeper, toward the spot where I had seen the flash of gold. I'd never imagined when I started the day that I would find myself wading in a lake, seeking out something I couldn't explain, all because of a feeling.

The water was getting higher, to the point I would soon have to dive under. I shivered as the sun peeked through a cluster of branches, again cutting into the water. There it was. The shiny object.

Here goes nothing.

Holding my breath, I ducked under, and a quick gasp escaped. Dang, it was cold, searing my skin in pinpricks. Wasting not a second more, I dove to the bottom, easily spotting the tiny trinket sitting on a bed of sand and shells. A halo of light beamed like a beacon. I reached out my fingers, clasping them around the object, and turned to kick off the bottom. A tide of water rushed over my face, carrying with it a song like a thousand mermaids singing. It surrounded me from all sides, seeming to carry me deeper into the lake.

I should have been scared, freaked out of my goddamn gourd, but I wasn't. Just the opposite. I was glowing, bathed in a soft blue light that carried a warmth of protection, like a bubble. And I found an ease in my lungs, allowing me to breathe underwater.

What the hell?

I paused in the center of the lake, my feet paddling in the water to keep me afloat, and through the blue mist surrounding me were faces

—beautiful women who looked like goddesses, draped in crowns and jewels. They were physically there, but as if they were part of the water.

Your time has come, daughter of goddess Styx. Their voices spoke as one unified, powerful voice. *Your awakening is upon you, and we welcome you into the fold, like our mothers before us. We are your sisters, Mallory, and this is our gift to you.*

What gift? The ring I had plucked from the bottom of the lake? This had to be some kind of hallucination, didn't it? Maybe the water was poisoned.

But the *gift* they were speaking of made itself known quickly.

A blinding flash of light exploded in the water. My ears throbbed, and I lost all sense of direction, unable to pinpoint the surface. The lake whirled in a mad blur, an insanity of color and intense coldness.

If this was the kind of gift they were offering me, I didn't want it.

Time didn't seem to exist in the lake, and I thought I might have passed out for a moment or two, but as reality slowly returned, I heard a voice, one I was certain I recognized.

Mallory! Mallory, can you hear me?

Yes, stop yelling. I hear you, I responded, or maybe I had in my head. It wasn't clear.

Mallory! Open your eyes.

Someone shook my shoulders, jostling me, and with effort, I peeled my eyes open. My vision was blurred as if I was looking through layers of gauze, but a dark face eventually materialized.

"Torent?"

In a rush of sensations, the world came flooding back, the sound of the waterfall crashing in the bluffs, the crisp, clear air mixed with hints of evergreens and Torent's cologne, and the coldness that reached deep into my soul.

I was no longer in the water, but on the grassy shore. Torent had pulled me out and was sitting beside me. I was shivering, teeth chattering together.

"W-what happened?" I stammered, searching Torent's face for answers. My heart knocked in my chest at the sight of him dripping wet, his T-shirt plastered against every muscle in his stomach.

"Are you crazy?" he reprimanded, brushing the strands of hair stuck to my face, before framing my cheeks with his hands.

"I saw something in the lake," I chattered, trying to keep my teeth together.

"And you thought it would be a good idea to jump in and get it?" Disapproval dripped in his voice, and it made me recoil.

I tried to scoot away from him, but his fingers slipped from my face to intertwine with my own, keeping me rooted. Dropping my gaze, I stared at our joined hands. They . . . they were glowing, like a mini aurora borealis. Umm . . .

"Why are our hands glowing?" I replied in a daze.

"What?" Torent's eyes moved downward as he noticed the splash of lights in hues of pink, blue, and green, just like the northern lights. "What the—" He released my fingers immediately as if I'd just burned him, extinguishing the light.

A sadness and longing overcame me. I missed it and reached to take his hand again, but Torent stood. I frowned, meeting his eyes.

They were dark, with little flecks of gold. "Oh no, crash car. No touching. Not until I figure out what is going on."

That made two of us. I sighed. "Fair enough. I went in to get this."

Opening my palm, I showed him the dainty gold ring. An engraving was etched into the band, words I couldn't read. They looked ancient. Encrusted into the center was a garnet stone that pulsed with energy. It was mesmerizing. I held it up between my thumb and index finger, watching as the sun bled over the horizon, catching the crystals.

"Is that—?" Torent knelt beside me again to get a closer look. He lifted his hand to take the ring, but the moment our fingers touched, I was transported to a different time, a different place. The only common denominator was Torent.

In moonlight and shadows of the woods, he kissed me. His lips were soft, and I closed my eyes, falling into the warmth that was all him. My body slipped up against his, quivering as he deepened the kiss, our tongues tangled in a dance. Emotion poured inside me until I ached with it.

Losing the last thread on my control, my hands shoved into his dark, silky hair, and I pulled him closer still. My lips glided over his jaw and down the strong column of his throat to where a pulse beat in time with my own. I flicked my tongue out, feeling the thrill of making it quicken.

Something passed between Torent and me, a power I couldn't explain.

Those crystal-violet eyes fired like flames.

And then it was gone, as quickly as it had manifested.

The vision, or whatever that had been, might have faded, but the feel of his lips, the taste of him lingered, as did the way he made me feel. I stared at Torent, fighting the desire to plead with him to kiss me.

"What are you doing here? Are you following me?" I finally asked when I trusted myself to speak. My voice was raspy, and the sound made my cheeks blush, because I knew he understood why.

"No," he replied, staring at me in a way that made my heart race. "It was a good thing I found you."

He was no longer touching me, and the ring was safely in my palm. I wasn't sure why that mattered. "Okay, stalker."

His lips twitched as he pushed to his feet. "Do I need to remind you that I saved you?"

I followed, standing, and was glad to find my legs were no longer shaking, not after that I-could-live-off-his-lips vision kiss . . . or whatever it had been. There seemed to be a lot of unexplained things happening to me, and it made me wonder if this entire day was nothing but a dream.

"Oh, are you expecting a thank you? For your information, I wasn't in any danger." Or so I thought.

He snorted. "We can argue about that later. First, we need to get warm before we both freeze to death. It's a decent hike, and unless you want to spend the night out here, you need to move your pretty little ass."

The urge to tell him to stop bossing me around rose up swiftly, but I couldn't fault his advice. Cold and wet was not a good combination. The anger was good, though; it kept the blood flowing.

"Do you know where you're going?" I called after his back. He had stepped up onto the embankment and paused, waiting for me to follow. Who would have thought Torent Stark could be a gentleman?

He rolled his eyes. "I've lived here all my life. There is no part of Havenwood Falls I haven't unearthed. How did you even find Peacock Lake?" he asked, giving me a hand up, but he made sure to quickly release me.

We both felt the spark, a thousand times more intense than before, and we both pretended otherwise.

I wasn't going to tell him I had gotten lost and stumbled on it accidentally; then again, maybe I hadn't. Just maybe, this place had summoned me to it.

"This isn't the falls?" I inquired.

He shook his head, dark damp strands of hair stuck to his forehead.

"No, this is Small's Falls. Peacock Lake is rumored to have magical qualities," he added.

I angled my head to the side, arms hugged around my middle to keep warm. "And you believe that?"

"After what just happened, you don't?" he asked, surprised.

Leaves of gold, red, and orange crunched under our feet as we entered the woods. "I don't know. What exactly did happen?"

Torent's deep violet eyes roamed over my face with traces of sympathy, an emotion I hadn't been sure he was capable of. "I think you need to ask your mom."

Confusion set in. "What does she have to do with this?"

"It's time you knew who you really are, Mal. Ask her. There's a reason you were drawn here. I don't think you finding Peacock Lake was an accident. And be careful with the ring. There's something about it that feels . . . off."

What did he mean who I really was?

I pocketed the little gold band, not giving it another thought.

CHAPTER 6

"*W*here's Mom?" I asked Gigi.

Gigi was in the kitchen, baking a batch of chocolate chip brownies. My favorite. "Out looking for a job, hopefully."

I sighed, sinking into one of the wooden kitchen chairs. My mind was still whirling and hadn't stopped the whole drive home.

Gigi gave me a sideways glance. "Why are you dripping water all over my hardwood floors? Nice T-shirt, by the way. Is it new?"

There she went again with her eerie intuition. She probably knew it was Torent's, so what was the point in lying? When we had gotten into his Jeep, he had thrown me a shirt from the backseat, ordering me to put it on. "I borrowed it."

"Why?" she pressed, beads of worry starting to form in her soft aqua eyes, the same color as mine.

"I went to the falls, or what I thought was the falls. Turns out, I ended up at Peacock Lake instead."

An interested gleam came into her expression before she went back to stirring the flour into her batter. "Did you, now? And did you find what you were looking for?"

The ring was in my pocket, but that wasn't what was on my mind.

"Gigi, I . . ." My voice trailed off. I didn't know how to put into words what had happened to me, not when I wasn't even sure myself.

She set aside the bowl and joined me at the table, taking my hand in her soft one. "It's okay, Mallory. I understand."

I raised my brows. How could she? I hadn't even said anything yet. "Do you?"

"Yes, my dear. This won't make your mother happy, but I can sense the power in you. This is your birthright. You've had your awakening today."

That was what the voices had said. Awakening. "What does that mean? What power? What birthright?"

"This is going to be hard to understand at first, but I want you to keep an open mind. You've always been so good at accepting the unexplained, unlike your mother. She was such a pistol, always challenging everything." She squeezed my hand. "You're a nymph."

I let out a little laugh. "I'm sorry, what did you say?"

"Just take a minute to think about it, really think about you, what calls to your soul. It has always been the water, hasn't it?"

I nodded. But I'm sure there were tons of people who liked to swim. I didn't think that made them mermaids.

"Havenwood Falls isn't just any place. It is a home for many supernaturals, including water nymphs like us," she explained.

Hold up a second. Gigi was a water nymph? Did that mean . . . ? My mouth dropped. How could that be possible? I was beginning to wonder if Gigi was off her rocker. Maybe she was sick. Water nymphs? Really? I shook my head. "That can't be."

She smiled in a reassuring gesture that was calming. "I think you know that I wouldn't make up something like this. Why do you think your mother took you from Havenwood Falls? She got it stuck in her head that she could protect you from this life. But you can't run from destiny, Mallory. And this is yours."

"Is Mom a . . . ?" I couldn't bring myself to say it.

Gigi's lips thinned. "Yes, she is, though she would rather not be."

So that was the big secret Mom had been running away from?

Suddenly all the pieces of my life started to fit into place. Holy fricking Toledo.

"I can't believe it," I groaned, laying my forehead on the table.

"It is a lot to take in," she said.

I lifted my head, trying to contain the storm of emotions swirling inside me. Anger. Betrayal. Confusion. Denial. Hurt. Bewilderment. "Why wouldn't she tell me? Why would she keep it a secret for so long?"

"Your mother's powers have brought her pain, and she wanted to protect you from ever getting hurt, but what she couldn't understand was your path is your own. It isn't your mother's to control or save you from."

I shook my head, still in a daze. "What kind of powers?"

"We don't share the same abilities, other than the call of the water. Our powers are a gift from the goddess and are as unique as our fingerprints. No two are identical."

Did I believe this? Gigi had no reason to lie to me, but still . . . "And there are others like us?"

"Many. And there will be time to learn everything you need to know, but I won't overwhelm you. First, you need to absorb what you've discovered about yourself. Controlling your ability is important. There are classes that can help you, but there is one rule I need you to absolutely understand. The humans can't know what you can do."

This was one of those moments in my life where I didn't know whether to laugh, cry, or run straight for the hills. But I had promised myself I wouldn't be Mom, and that was exactly what she had done.

"I don't even know what I can do," I whispered, staring at the dark grain spots in the kitchen table.

"You will," Gigi assured. "I'm here to help you. Always. But I need you to promise me you will keep this a secret. No one must know unless you're a hundred percent sure they're supernatural."

That might be kind of hard, since Torent more or less had been a witness to my awakening, but he hadn't freaked out. So I couldn't help but wonder. What was Torent? Human or supernatural?

"The Court takes these things very seriously. When your mom

42

called about coming home, I had to ask the Court for permission to remind your mom how to get here."

"Is that why you came to visit?"

She nodded. "It was the only way."

"I have a million questions."

"I know you do, but I think it would be best if you talk to your mom. She has strong feelings about your heritage."

Those feelings had been strong enough to keep me from this place for seventeen years. "Thanks, Gigi, for being straight with me. It's been a very long and confusing day. I'm going to lie down until Mom gets home."

She patted my hand. "Good idea. I'll bring you up a bowl of hot brownies and ice cream."

Because that would make everything better.

I stood up, feeling numb all over.

Gigi wrapped me in a hug. "I'll send your mom upstairs the moment she walks through the door. You should be the one to tell her."

Holy crap. I was a freaking water nymph.

I hurried upstairs to my still unpacked room and immediately opened my laptop. Time to dive into the deep dark web. Or Google, in my case. As expected, it took ten years to boot up. I could have gotten a manicure in the time it took.

Pulling up the search engine, I typed in the words *water nymph.*

As I stared at the computer, it hit me. I wasn't human. How could I have not known my whole life? Tears I didn't want gathered at the corners of my eyes. *Nope. I'm not going to cry.*

The basic info came up. Greek mythology, a nature deity that presided over bodies of water. Okay, the idea of being a deity was kind of badass.

Then I searched *goddess Styx.* The voices in the water had said I was the daughter of goddess Styx. From my mythology class last year, I knew a little bit about Styx, the goddess of the underworld river who was the personification of hatred. That didn't sound promising. As I dug deeper, I found out her parents were Oceanus

43

and Tethys. She became the divinity by whom most solemn oaths were sworn.

I wasn't sure what any of this had to do with me or how much of her power was passed down through our bloodline.

Remembering the ring I had found, I slipped it out of my pocket to examine it. The metal was cool against my fingers as I held it up, twisting it under the soft glow of the bedside lamp. The garnet caught the light, and I swore the stone swirled in a cloudy pattern, but that was crazy. Maybe it was one of those mood rings?

Without thinking, I slipped it onto my finger, surprised to find it was a perfect fit. The whirling inside the ruby intensified, like red clouds during a blood moon. I stared, drawn to the allure it produced. I felt pulled in, and in the clouds, flashes of Torent and me spun inside my head. Steamy. Sexy. Sinister.

I flipped off the ring and quickly dropped it inside the nightstand drawer. Out of sight, out of mind.

Holy crap. I couldn't even process what had just happened. My breath came out in short pants, and my body! My skin was on fire. What was going on? Was this part of my powers, having over-the-top-erotic visions of stupid hot guys? If that was the case, being a nymph sucked.

Before I spontaneously combusted, I dropped down on my bed and closed my eyes. Flashes of being underwater flipped through my mind. If Torent hadn't been there, would I be alive?

Maybe I owed him a thank you after all. If supernaturals were real, then what was Torent?

Definitely not human.

MOM and I had our little talk that night everything changed, and I suddenly found myself enrolled in supernatural night classes at Sun and Moon Academy two days a week. I wasn't thrilled about the extra work. It would mean less time for swimming and studying, but I couldn't deny I was a tiny bit excited. As scary as it had been to learn I was supernatural, I was also extremely curious. Knowledge had always been my thing. I liked to learn, and this was no different.

After everything that had happened over the weekend, I needed to unwind, and as much as I loved the water, I wasn't eager to jump in just yet. The Creekwood Country Club had a great space inside a small room of the workout center that was perfect for yoga. I had seen something about yoga classes at the local vineyard, but Beck preferred solo versus group settings. He had convinced me to meet him here after school, assuring that what I needed was the mental, physical, and spiritual discipline of yoga. He was right about one thing. I needed to Zen out more than ever. Plus, I was having the Monday blues.

Starting without Beck, I moved into the resting position of downward dog, concentrating on the ins and outs of my breath. It didn't last more than a minute.

"Nice spandex."

I peered under my armpit at Torent scowling.

"Is there a reason you're interrupting my thirty minutes of peace?" How was this guy everywhere I turned? Was there no place in Havenwood Falls safe from Torent Stark?

His head was angled to the side, and our gazes locked. The depths of his violet eyes glimmered with a magic that could hypnotize. I had no other explanation. "This is what you call peace? I'm still trying to figure out how you're going to get out of that pose without breaking your neck."

I rolled my eyes and dropped down to my knees. "I'm assuming this is about the other day?"

The day I found out I wasn't human. I was still waiting for someone to pinch me and tell me my life had suddenly become a fantasy novel.

His lips spread into a roguish grin. "Nah, I came to appreciate the view."

I ignored the comment, knowing a reaction would only feed his ego, so I took a different approach. "I know I didn't say it then, but thank you for stalking me the other day."

He folded his arms. "Wow."

"What?" I asked, pushing myself to my feet.

"That looked like it hurt. The thank you," he added, in case it wasn't clear, which it had been.

"Shut up. You can be such an ass sometimes, you know that?"

His unusual eyes twinkled. "So I've been told."

And he liked it. "Are you sure it's safe for you to be seen with me here? We wouldn't want to upset the queen."

He winked, taking a step closer to me. "I scoped the place out first. We're in the clear."

My bare feet sank into the foam yoga mat as realization hit. We were utterly alone. "How do you keep showing up everywhere I am? I'm really starting to think you're a stalker."

"The town really isn't that big."

Sad excuse. "So what's the reason you interrupted my practice? I assume there's a reason."

He leaned forward and tucked a stray piece of hair behind my ear. I pretended not to notice how his fingers lingered over my cheek. "Have dinner with me Friday night."

I couldn't ignore the flush that stole over my cheeks. The simple brush of touch ignited a trail of warm embers at the side of my face.

"No," I refused. Me and Torent alone, even in a restaurant, was a dangerous cocktail. It wasn't just his crazy ex-or-non-ex-girlfriend that had me wary of the youngest Stark. It was mostly because I didn't trust myself with him. I could close my eyes right now and still feel what it was like to be in his arms, to kiss him. The vision I'd had at the waterfall had been so real, and yet, it never happened. I wasn't about to tempt fate.

No guys. Remember?

But he was persistent. "We need to talk about what happened."

He wasn't the only one who could be stubborn to a fault. "What if I don't want to?"

"Mallory." He used my full name. Not Mal. Not crash car. Which meant he was being serious.

I sighed. It would be nice to talk to someone other than family, but I remembered the rule. Keep it a secret from humans. I didn't know where Torent stood on the spectrum. Supe or not? "Fine. But no funny business."

"Just so we're clear . . ." He dipped his chin, and the wind shifted directions through the open window, blowing Torent's scent straight at me. I told myself not to breathe, but I inhaled, drawing in the smell of pine and mint. It was all Torent. I wanted to bury my face into his neck, wrap my arms around his broad shoulders, and stay surrounded by his warmth, because lately, I was so cold. "No hand-holding . . ." His fingers laced gently with mine, sending a warm spark down my arm. "No whispering in your ear . . ." He had leaned close, letting his breath fan over my ear. "And definitely no kissing." His lips hovered over mine.

I drew on every ounce of willpower and stepped back, the soft glow that had started to form vanishing. "All of the above counts as funny business."

He gave me a lopsided grin that was all trouble. "If you say so."

Something happened each time Torent touched me, and I was going out on a limb when I added, "Also, one more thing."

He raised a single brow.

I took a breath. "You have to tell me what you are."

He opened his mouth, but then shut it, pressing his lips together. "I'll pick you up at six."

Shit. Please don't let me regret this.

CHAPTER 7

"*D*id I just hear Torent Stark ask you out?" Beck asked, finally showing up. He was supposed to meet me twenty minutes ago.

I wasn't mad and couldn't decide if his being late was a blessing in disguise or a nightmare. "Unfortunately, yes."

Beck scratched his blueberry-colored head. "Strange, because I thought I heard you agree."

I sighed. "I did."

Wearing sweatpants and a T-shirt, Beck dropped his mat to the floor, tsking his tongue. "Girl, you have a death wish. Brooklyn is going to go apeshit."

"Probably," I agreed. What had I gotten myself into? I should have stuck with my initial no, but damn Torent and his violet eyes. And damn those stupid visions for making me wonder if his lips really tasted as hot in person, or if it was just my imagination gone wild.

Beck turned his eyes on me, studying me with a critical gaze. "You look different. What's going on with you?"

"I do?" I squeaked, looking guilty as hell.

Beck's eyes swept over me from head to toe. "Yeah. You're glowing."

"It must be the yoga," I mumbled, shifting my weight to one foot. His intuitive scrutiny was making me nervous.

He wasn't buying it. Beck placed his thumb on his bottom lip. "I've been in touch with all my chakras and never looked that radiant."

"I had a strange weekend."

"That pretty much sums up every weekend here in Havenwood Falls."

"I'm beginning to figure that out."

Beck lifted a brow. "Really? Do you want to elaborate?"

Did I? Beck was really my only friend in Havenwood Falls, but could I trust him to keep a secret of this magnitude? I really, really wanted to tell him, like it was killing me to keep this secret inside me, but I was also afraid. Rule number one: Never tell humans what you were. Right now, I wanted Beck to be supernatural.

"Not yet," I sighed.

Beck struck me as the kind of friend who was okay with me not being ready to talk about what was going on with me. It was one of the many reasons I liked him. He was dependable. I could count on him. I definitely needed a friend like that in my life.

WEDNESDAY AFTER SCHOOL I was scheduled to get my official tattoo that registered me as a supernatural. My talk with mom had enlightened me on some of the inner workings of life in Havenwood Falls for people like us. I was blown away by what went on in the town right under the noses of everyone else.

I had mixed feelings about being required to get inked, mostly because I didn't feel as if I'd had enough time to digest who I was. My magic was still in an unstable zone, but that was part of the classes at the Academy, to help me learn to control it. My life hadn't moved past the movie quality. None of it seemed real.

But that needle jabbing into my skin . . . that would feel very real.

"Have you picked out what you want to represent you?" Mom asked. She was tidying up the house before Addie arrived. Mom liked cleaning about as much as I liked anchovies. It made her ill, but was the life of a parent.

I gnawed on my lower lip as I wiped down the kitchen table. "I think so."

"Where are you going to put it?" she asked, loading the last of the breakfast bowls into the dishwasher.

"Don't laugh."

"Why would I laugh?"

I gave her a dull glare.

She held up her hands, dripping water all over the floor, and made a cross over her heart. "I swear."

"My ear."

Her lips straightened in a thin line. "That is going to hurt, honey. Like a lot."

Could always count on words of encouragement from Mom. "No pain, no gain."

She returned her hands into the water. "That's my girl. You always were a tough cookie, regardless of your fear of needles."

I put the cleaning supplies under the sink and leaned on the counter beside her. "Can we skip the trip down memory lane?"

The sound of tires crunching over gravel floated in through the open window. Addie had arrived. Mom shut off the water and wiped her hands on the dishtowel. "Can you get the door?"

I nodded and pushed off the counter to make my way down the hall. The bell rang right before I got to the door. *Here goes nothing.* This was it. No denying what I was. With a sigh, I opened the door.

Addie Beaumont was the Court of the Sun and the Moon's business manager. She had pretty light brown hair and warm chocolate eyes behind black-framed glasses. Tattoos adorned both her arms, and her fingers glittered with enough rings for a gypsy.

I instantly liked her, and considering she would be the one holding the needle gun, that was a comforting thing.

"You ready for this?" she asked, the little diamond stud in her nose twinkling.

She followed me down the hall, back into the kitchen. "Is anyone really ready to be assaulted by a rapid needle gun?"

She chuckled, and it was a pleasant sound. "Good point, but I promise I'll be gentle, and it will be over before you know it."

While I pulled my hair back into a messy bun, Mom and Addie exchanged a polite hello. I showed Addie where I wanted the tattoo.

"Really?" she said lifting a brow. "That is totally bitchin'."

I grinned. Hell yeah. I could be bitchin' if I wanted.

Addie set up her supplies on the table and took a moment to sketch the design with a black pen on my ear. This was the easy part. Mom pulled a chair over beside me and held my hand. "Try not to pass out."

"Mom," I groaned, rolling my eyes.

"Could you add a protection charm?" Mom asked Addie.

I glanced over at her, curious why she would ask for protection. What did I need protection from? But I figured now wasn't the best time to grill her for answers, in front of a guest. I didn't want to embarrass Mom, although she had no problem embarrassing me.

Addie gave a short nod. "Of course."

The buzzing of the tattoo gun brought my drifting thoughts to a sobering end. It was the moment of truth.

I forced myself to breathe in and out of my nose like I was meditating.

"Do you want me to numb the pain?" Addie asked, seeing my face pale. The needle dipped in black ink and was hovering to the right of my ear.

I shook my head and squeezed my hands over my knees. "I'm okay." My heartbeat sounded rapidly in my ears.

Addie gave me a soft smile. "Good, now remember to keep still. I wouldn't want to accidentally tat your cheek."

I closed my eyes, and an image of Torent's face appeared, followed by a ribbon of calmness. The first pierce shot a zing through my ear, but it didn't take long for it to go numb. The whole thing took less than fifteen minutes, and I couldn't believe I had made such a big deal about it.

Mom took care of the registry and the supernatural details I knew virtually nothing about while I admired my new piece of body art in the portable mirror. A series of swirls climbed up the lobe of my ear and curved toward the top.

"Let me see," Mom sung.

I angled my head to the side.

"It's official. She's one of us now," Addie said, smiling.

Mom brushed at her eyes. "Yes, she is."

A pang hit me in the heart. It hurt to see her sad, and I wasn't entirely sure why it upset her so much, seeing me embrace my heritage.

FRIDAY NIGHT CAME TOO QUICKLY. My not-date with Torent.

I stared at the muscles in Torent's arm as he turned the wheel, taking us onto the main road. He was wearing a hoodie with the sleeves pushed up. The black ink of his tattoo was embedded in his golden skin, and I found the sight of the interwoven symbol attractive on him. An urge to trace the lines with my finger snuck up on me, and I had to lace my hands together to keep from touching him.

My eyes moved up to the profile of his face. It was a striking face —cheekbones I could get hung up on, eyes I could lose myself in, and lips I wanted to kiss again and again.

He turned to catch me gawking and let his dimples come out to play. "You don't have to stop staring. I like it."

I snorted. "You would like it." I turned to watch the breathtaking landscape roll by. It was almost as enchanting as the guy beside me. "What does your tattoo mean?" I asked, directing the conversation to a safe topic.

His gaze slid back to the road. It was pretty much a straight shot to town. "What makes you think it has a meaning?"

"Isn't that the whole point of getting one in the first place?" I pressed, unable to believe he got something so permanent for the hell of it, but then again, that was the kind of guy Torent was.

He shrugged. "To some. But for people like us, it is a requirement."

"What do you mean, people like us?" I tossed back with a slight edge in my voice.

The corners of his lips curved.

"Supernaturals," he said, as if it was the most natural answer in the world.

My shock face materialized, and I sucked in a sharp breath, fingers tightening painfully together. So I had been right, but it didn't make my surprise any less real.

"Are you supposed to say that out loud?" I whispered, my gaze darting out the windows.

He chuckled. "No one can hear us, Mal. We're in a car. Okay, that's not exactly true," he backpedaled. "There are some supes who have enhanced hearing, but it is unlikely they're around."

"Should we even be talking about this? Isn't it a—?"

"Secret," he supplied. "Don't worry. You're not going to get in trouble." Swinging his Jeep into a parking space, he shifted it into park.

My eyes narrowed. "And why should I trust you?"

Torent killed the engine and turned to face me, locking his gaze on mine. "You shouldn't . . . but when it comes to your safety, I wouldn't put you in harm."

My heart cartwheeled. Why did he say stuff like that to me?

Together we climbed out of the jeep.

"I hope you like pizza," Torent said when we met at the front of his car.

I scrunched my face. "Is there anyone who doesn't?"

His lips twitched. "I knew I liked you for a reason."

My stupid heart did another acrobatic move. *Big deal. He said he liked you. That could mean a thousand things, including friends,* I reminded myself.

Napoli's was a local pizzeria in a brick building across from the fire station. A large window with a green and white canopy welcomed its patrons. Inside, the place was lively with locals and a few kids from school. Torent gave a short nod in the direction of one table before we were seated.

I slid into the booth opposite Torent, the gently worn leather soft underneath me. It was obvious the town loved this place. The air smelled of gooey cheese, zesty tomato sauce, and garlic. Everything *I* loved. Pizza was life.

"Hey, Zara," Torent greeted the waitress. I recognized her from school. She had amazing olive-toned skin and features that reminded me of an elf.

"The usual?" she directed at him with a cute British accent.

"What do you like on your pizza?" Torent turned and asked me.

I unfolded the menu on the table to keep my hands busy. "The question you should be asking is what don't I like on my pizza."

His smile was lethal. "The usual, thanks, Zara."

Don't get hung up on him.

"Did you take my advice and talk to your mom?" he asked as soon as Zara had left to put in our order, not beating around the bush.

My eyes met his. "It was my grandma who told me."

"And what did she say?" A kind of ridicule dusted his voice, and I wondered why.

Zara returned, setting our drinks on the table. I drew a long sip from the Coke. Was this really the place to have the kind of discussion I agreed to?

"Why do I have to go first?" I challenged, putting the ball in his court. I wasn't ready to reveal my cards just yet. Call me cautious.

"Fine, have it your way, but be warned, you might not like what you learn."

"I can handle it," I assured him, twisting the straw around in my drink. Couldn't I? How bad could it be? Vampire? Werewolf?

He leaned forward on the table, closing us in so we were in our own little bubble. "My father is a higher demon."

CHAPTER 8

"*A* demon," I hissed. The fork and knife in front of me began to tremble, moving toward me on the table. I quickly slapped my hand down over them, feeling a charge of energy in my veins. *Holy crap.* I had done that.

Torent's eyes shifted over the pizzeria, checking to see if anyone was paying us any attention. "You're going to need to work on your control, but it is normal to be unstable at first, so don't freak out."

Who was freaking out? Certainly not me.

"Humans, they don't know about us," he continued. "And we need to keep it that way. It's one of the laws enforced by the Court of the Sun and the Moon."

I stared at him across the table, seeing him in a different light. *A demon*, my brain echoed. I had the hots for a demon. "I'm sorry, what did you say?"

He reclined back into the booth, the corner of his mouth tipping up. "You have so much to learn, crash car."

I sighed, tapping my foot under the table. "This is insane."

"Insane doesn't begin to cover Havenwood Falls."

A group of guys and girls stopped at our table. I didn't recognize any of their faces, but it was clear they knew Torent. Both of the guys were dressed in jeans, white T-shirts, and motorcycle jackets. The two girls were cute. One had lavender hair I would have died for, and the other had deep brown eyes accentuated by bold turquoise eyeshadow.

"Hey, where you been, Stark? You missed our last get together," said one of the guys. He was tall with piercing blue eyes and had a scar just above his right eye that added to his deadly charm.

"Been kind of busy," Torent replied, laying a lazy arm over the back of the booth.

Those roguish blues turned to me. "I can see that. I don't think we've met before. I never forget a pretty face."

Torent scowled. "Mallory, this is River Livingston III, Rowan Bishop, Julianna Fairchild, and Zaltana Purser."

"Hi," I said, at a loss for words. If they knew Torent, did that mean they were supes? I had to bite my lip to keep the question from blurting out.

"What is a nice girl like you doing with the likes of Torent Stark?" Zaltana asked me.

I liked her boldness. "I'm still trying to figure that out."

"Catch up with us later, Pallas," River said to Torent. "And you'd better graduate this year."

He watched as the group moved to a few booths behind us to take a seat. I could easily imagine Torent hanging out with those guys and getting into all kinds of trouble in town.

I lifted a brow. "Pallas? Like the Titan god?"

The corner of his lips lifted a fraction. "It's just a nickname."

Odd nickname.

Tucking my hair behind my ears, I stared at the wrinkles frowning over his forehead. "What did he mean, you'd better graduate?"

He gave a one-shoulder shrug. "Long story short, last year I screwed around, skipped classes, basically blew off my entire senior year of school. I didn't have enough credits to graduate, so I'm stuck doing another semester at HFH."

"They went to Havenwood Falls High?" I inquired.

Torent shook his head. "River and Rowan went to the Academy. The others went to HFH."

"Oh. I'm taking night classes there this week."

The sudden harshness that moved into his face startled me. "Mal, just promise you'll be careful."

His hand reached across the table and covered mine.

I glanced down, seeing the stream of colors starting to take shape as his fingers absently twisted the gold ring I had thrown on at the last second. I wasn't even sure why I wore it, but the metal seemed to warm the second Torent touched me. "Why does that happen when we touch? Is it normal?"

He snatched his hand away before anyone could notice. Those troubled stormy eyes followed mine. "No. Not even by supe standards, but I've been doing some research. You must have gotten some kind of magnetic powers from the water currents, and it reacts to the energy inside me."

The burning sensation that started as a spark in my chest bloomed, spreading throughout my veins. "So you're saying when our powers collide, they give off something that looks like the aurora borealis."

He nodded. "Yeah, I think so."

I shook my fingers, trying to rid myself of the lingering tingle and the urge to reconnect our hands. "Have you ever seen anything like this before?"

The scowl that formed on his kissable lips deepened. "I've seen some pretty remarkable abilities, but no. It could be because I'm involved that makes it more surreal."

I got that.

"None of this seems real," I mumbled.

He lowered his eyes, thick lashes resting over his cheeks. "You're wearing the ring you found."

I shrugged like it wasn't a big deal, and I didn't think it was. "It's pretty. And it fits."

I had also been curious to see if I would have any other flashes of Torent and me doing dirty and wicked things.

"Do you feel that?" he asked, making sure to keep his hands on his side of the booth.

The urge to jump over the table and attack him with my mouth? Hell yes, I felt it, but I kept my composure. This insane pull inside me intensified, and I found myself leaning across the table. His eyes darkened as they collided with mine. The emotion churning in them had my breath quickening.

"Mallory." The husky sound of my name did all kinds of funny things to my belly.

My heart was thumping in my chest as my eyes focused on his. The air between us crackled, and I wanted more than anything to be anywhere but a public place with Torent.

Tearing his gaze from my fingers, he looked at me, and I didn't like what I saw brewing in the violet storm. "There is something about that ring."

For some reason, his tone covered me in a cloud of unease. "Do you want me to take it off?"

"No, I'm sure it's nothing." But the look on his face said the exact opposite.

"You don't really believe that."

His fingers kneaded the muscle at the back of his neck. "I don't know. I have this hunch, but I don't want to jump to conclusions until I ask around. Finding something at the bottom of Peacock Lake is risky."

"Because the lake is enchanted?" I concluded.

He nodded. "It is also fatal to humans. Your mom really never told you what you are?"

Sadness crept into my eyes, and I swallowed the lump of deceit. "No. How could she keep it from me?"

He shifted in the leather booth. "I don't know. But I'm sure she had her reasons, Mal. Probably to protect you from this place."

I fumbled with the edge of my white cloth napkin. "Is it really that bad to be supernatural?"

He bestowed me with a magnetic smirk that seemed to scatter my brain cells. "You're asking the wrong person. I'm a demon. Bad is my thing."

My lips twitched.

"I'm a water nymph, apparently," I said, realizing I hadn't gotten around to telling him.

"I figured as much, but wasn't a hundred percent sure."

"How did you know?" Was that something other supes noticed?

"I've been around a few others enough to pick up the signs."

The pizza arrived, and we tabled the discussion of supernaturals to talk about normal stuff. Turned out, Torent was easy to open up to. I didn't know what it was. Maybe I trusted him, which sounded crazy. I'd only been in Havenwood Falls a short time, and yet, my life had already been turned upside down.

We managed to eat the entire pizza between the two of us. Torent could pack it away, but you would never be able to tell by looking at him. How he remained so fit with an appetite like that I'd never figure out. Just one of those mysteries of life, or being a demon.

He took care of the check, overriding my insistence to let me pay for half. As we walked outside, I made him swear next time it would be on me.

In response, he raised his brows and asked, "So there's going to be a next time?"

I rolled my eyes.

"I haven't decided," I replied and jumped into his Jeep.

A bundle of nerves formed in my belly as we coasted along the road that was now becoming familiar. The butterflies came out of nowhere. Why was I suddenly so uneasy? All evening I'd been relaxed in his presence, and now that we were alone, I found I couldn't calm down. My fingers twisted around the ring.

"There's no reason to be nervous," Torent said as we pulled into my driveway and he killed the lights.

We both unbuckled our seatbelts. "I just learned you're a demon, and I'm not even sure what that means. I have an active imagination, so you can imagine the things that are running wild in there."

"Fair enough." He shifted comfortably in the seat, letting the engine idle in a rhythmic purr. "My mom is human, which makes my demon blood diluted. I don't have the intense power my father does. He can morph into a full-out demon. Don't piss the man off."

I chuckled, but it still had undertones of nerves. There were demons running around, and witches, shifters, and werewolves.

Holy crap.

That animal who had darted out in front of my car . . . it could have been a supe.

"My change is more subtle. I can produce a light called hellfire, and I got the demon eyes and senses."

The more I learned, the more intrigued I was. "Show me the demon eyes."

He lifted a brow at me. "You sure you can handle this?"

I smiled and folded my arms, angling my body toward him in the seat. "Show me," I insisted.

"Okay," he said, and I could sense his reluctance. In the moonlight, the car was dark, but I could see his violet eyes lit up by the dashboard lights. They were as beautiful and mesmerizing as ever, maybe more so in twilight. He took one long blink, and as his long lashes batted open, I gasped.

The entire car was bathed in a golden glow produced by his eyes. The violet color was replaced with vibrant orangey-yellow, like a large cat at night.

He had been expecting me to recoil, be scared even, but that wasn't what I was feeling when I stared at Torent. My hand reached out, tracing the soft lines of his jaw, and something stirred deep within me. My nervous demeanor calmed the moment I touched him.

"They're stunning."

His exhale filled the quiet car, a breath I didn't know he'd been holding. It was followed by a crooked smile on his full lips. Then came the dimples. My heart seemed to stutter as Torent lowered his head, resting his forehead against mine.

"You surprise me," he murmured.

Time seemed to stand still, the seconds stretching out as I stared into his eyes, watching them darken. My hand was still on his face, and I couldn't seem to move it. "Me? I'm the most predictable, boring—"

He kissed me. No, that wasn't quite the way to describe his lips pressed to mine. It was more than a kiss.

He possessed me.

There wasn't a second of hesitation. I wish I could have said the same, but the moment Torent's lips pressed against mine, thought ceased to be available. A shudder raked through his body, and my own answered at the sound of a part growl, half moan at the back of his throat.

I closed the tiny space between us and kissed him with every ounce of fervor in my body. I had no self-control, it seemed. Kissing Torent under the stars was the last thing I should have been doing. My life had enough drama. I didn't need to add to it. And yet, here I was, slipping my fingers into his hair as my body instinctually relaxed into his.

Parting my lips, I deepened the kiss. Something cool and metallic slipped between our tongues as his tangled with mine in a dance as old as time. I could feel myself come alive under his fingers when they dove into my hair. What he made me feel was both thrilling and frightening.

He pulled his lips from mine, tilting his head to the side, and stared at me in wonder. A strand of dark hair fell, teasing his high cheekbone.

"I've never kissed someone with a pierced tongue," I whispered, gazing into his vibrant gold eyes.

A wicked gleam jumped into them. "I'm full of surprises, crash car."

I just bet he was, and if I didn't get out of this car, I would end up in his lap. Kissing Torent in the flesh had been a thousand times more potent than the visions. I didn't know what to make of that yet.

Flashing him a smile, I opened my door and stepped out of the Jeep. "Thanks for dinner. And listening to me." He was the only person besides my family who knew what I was. It had been nice having someone to relate to.

I would never have thought that person would have been Torent.

I just hoped my secret was safe with him.

CHAPTER 9

*H*oly crap. I kissed Torent.

I was having one of those squealing moments, and it felt as if I floated upstairs to my room. The house was quiet, Mom and Gigi in their rooms watching TV or reading.

After taking a quick shower, I texted Beck, letting him know how my not-date with Torent had gone, and climbed into bed. I fumbled with the garnet ring on my finger, telling myself what happened between Torent and me tonight was not a big deal. I wasn't going to let it go to my head. The plan was still in place, and no demon with sexy dimples would derail me.

I fell asleep with a smile on my lips.

That kiss sparked something in my sleep.

He was sleeping in his bed, a beam of moonlight slashing across his face. I'd never been to his house, let alone in his bedroom, but I knew, without doubt, this was exactly what it would look like.

What was I doing in his room?

Unable to stop myself, I padded over to his bed and crawled in beside him. What had gotten into me?

But he rolled over in his sleep, and my mouth was on his. The action seemed to have caught him off guard, but only for a second, because then his lips were moving over mine, taking me somewhere wild and electric.

It wasn't enough, just kissing him. I needed more. I needed to go deeper. I needed to taste him, feel him.

My fingers slipped under the sheets, and I moaned, finding he wasn't wearing a shirt. Of course, Torent would sleep in nothing but boxers. God bless him.

I ran my tongue over his lower lip and whispered his name. Torent opened his eyes, and my breath caught. They were no longer a stunning shade of purple, but a fiery gold.

"The ring," he growled.

MY EYES FLEW open as I wrenched upright in my bed, my heart beating rapidly in my chest. I ran my fingers through my tousled hair, the blankets twisted around me.

What the hell was that?

It felt like a ghost had brushed over my soul. I wrapped my arms around myself and stared into the dark. It was then I noticed the ring on my hand. The garnet stone was glowing, pulsing like the beat of a heart.

I ripped the ring from my finger, casting it aside on the nightstand.

ALL DAY, only one word ran through my head over and over again. *Supernaturals.* Something inside me had snapped, and now I couldn't stop staring at everyone, wondering if they were human or something else. It was the something else that was causing me to go crazy.

Oh, I knew what books and movies claimed, but this was real life —my life, and the girl next to me in AP English could be a vampire. The teacher in Physics could be a ghost. And my new best friend, Beck? I was pretty damn sure he was more than the adorable nerd with blue hair.

Maybe if I had wrapped my head around it, I wouldn't be

struggling so much, but the truth was, I hadn't. And the other night, I'd been locking lips with a demon.

Never thought that would be something I wanted to do . . . or do again.

Strange thing was, I did, and the dreams I kept having of him weren't helping.

Torent and I hadn't talked much since the kiss, and I told myself it wasn't that big of a deal. I didn't automatically assume he was my boyfriend and we'd be walking hand in hand down the hall, but I had at least expected him to say more than two words to me.

"Earth to Mallory."

I didn't know how many times Beck had called my name, but I pulled my gaze from outer space and looked at him on the treadmill next to mine. We were in the school's gym, getting our cardio on. Or trying to. I had been a million miles away. Why had I let Beck talk me into working out after school when all I wanted to do was go home and not think about kissing Torent? *Because you thought it would be a good distraction.* Joke was on me. "Sorry. Family stuff. I've got a lot on my mind."

Beck's brows drew together. He was barely breaking a sweat, and I hated him for it. "Well, that's not as interesting as what I thought you were thinking about. It was more like you and Torent getting hot and sticky over pizza."

Oh, my god. Did the entire school know we'd gone out? "It wasn't a date."

A hint of a smirk touched his lips. "That's not the word going around school."

"Beck," I groaned, trying to keep my balance on the walking machine. "You promised you wouldn't tell anyone."

He made a zipper motion across his lips. "Babe, these lips are sealed tighter than Fort Knox. It wasn't me."

Wonderful. That would explain why Brooklyn had been glaring extra hard at me all day. Even now, from across the gym. The damn girl looked good sweating. Her skin glistened. She was wearing a white tank top and a pair of pink shorts.

Is that a—?

Brooklyn had a tattoo.

Shit. Brooklyn was a supe?

My gaze darted back to Beck and the black ink on his neck. God, I was surrounded by supernaturals, and regardless of rule number one, I had to know if he was human or something else.

Didn't I?

"Can I ask you a question?" The words popped out of my mouth before I let myself overthink it.

Not missing a beat, Beck said, "Yes, I think you should have sex with Torent Stark."

I smiled. "Funny. Brooklyn Kendall might behead me. Besides, I haven't decided what I'm going to do about him, but that wasn't what I wanted to ask."

"Fire away."

Our running machines hummed in time together, our strides in unison. "You don't strike me as a tattoo type of guy. Why did you get one?"

Beck wasn't muscular, but he could run. "I didn't have a choice. You know, the rules."

Beads of sweat ran down my back as I gave him a funny look. "Are you saying . . . ?" I swallowed, unable to bring myself to say the word.

His eyes twinkled, enjoying my discomfort. "That I'm a shifter? I thought that was pretty clear."

My eyes darted around the gym fitness room. I was afraid someone might have heard him.

"Not to me, it isn't. This whole new world is confusing." I made sure to keep my voice low.

Holy smokes. My best friend shifted into an animal.

"Right, it's easy to forget you didn't grow up knowing. Why exactly didn't you know?" he asked.

I shrugged. "I honestly don't have any idea. My mom claims it was to protect me, but from what, I don't know. My dad, maybe?"

Beck peered over at me. "Who is he?"

"Another question I can't answer."

"Damn. That sucks, Mal."

"Tell me about it." I adopted my best indifferent tone, but the truth was, the curiosity about who my father was had never dulled, not since I was a little girl. I just did a better job of hiding it from Mom.

"Let's find out," Beck suggested, as if it were a simple thing.

"And how do you propose we do that, besides asking my mom, which I've done a hundred times already. She isn't budging."

"Do you have a name?"

"Yeah."

"And?" he prodded.

"Roth Dorian. I'm not sure this is a good idea," I added, but what was stopping me from taking the chance to find out any information about my mysterious father?

He eyed me. "What could it hurt?"

I hit the decline button on the treadmill, lowering my speed to a walk I could tolerate without my pits dripping. "I don't know, maybe. I actually have something else I wanted to ask you."

Beck lifted his brow as I suddenly had his undivided attention. "This sounds juicy."

I had to tell someone about the ring. Someone other than Torent. "When I was at Peacock Lake, I found something. A ring."

Scowl lines started to form over Beck's damp brow. "The day you came into your powers?"

I nodded. "There's something strange about it."

Beck tugged the plastic key out of his machine and let it roll to a stop. "Anything that comes out of Peacock Lake can't be good. Where is it?"

"I left it at home."

He grabbed a white towel that hung over the armrest on the treadmill and whipped it across his forehead. "What day do you have night school this week?"

"Thursday," I answered, wondering where this was going.

"Good. I'll meet you there. And bring the ring," he added.

"We're not going to get in trouble or anything?" I was a little taken aback at how forthcoming he was with supe information. He talked about this stuff like we were discussing the weather.

He winked. "Let me teach you the ropes, Mal."

"What kind of shifter are you?" I whispered.

His eyes did a weird glowy thing. Not quite like Torent's, but still eerie. "Wolf." Beck's eyes suddenly changed, hardening. "Don't look now, but I think you're about to get a visit from the bitch squad."

CHAPTER 10

*B*rooklyn sauntered up to my treadmill with her two sidekicks beside her and pulled out the safety key, letting it dangle from her finger as my machine stopped. "Well, if it isn't the late bloomer. Rumor has it you had quite the magical time last weekend."

Did she just make a remark about me being a nymph or was I reading too much into everything she said? It couldn't be.

"What do you want?" I asked her dryly, not in the mood. Way too much crap was going on in my head to deal with her on top of it all.

She stepped up so we were at eye level. I could count her eyelashes, we were that close. "I thought I had made myself clear."

"You're going to have to elaborate. I don't speak psycho ex-girlfriend babble."

She laughed, an evil sound that struck me in the gut. "Is that what he told you? That I was his ex-girlfriend? Torent and I, we understand each other. Where do you think he went after he dropped you off the other night? I can tell you it wasn't home."

I didn't believe it. She was just trying to get under my skin . . . and it was working, but I would keep my cool. I wasn't going to smear the smug smile off her face with the belt of the treadmill. "Why do I care where he goes?"

"Maybe you don't. But you might care about what he is saying about you."

Nope. I wasn't going to take the bait. *Don't do it.* My eyes bounced to her sidekicks, Leena and Cora, before returning to the devil herself. "I can see you're dying to tell me, so just spill it."

Brooklyn leaned forward, closing her hand over mine on the handle of the running machine.

"I know what you are," she whispered. Her hand reached out to grab my wrist, and the little devil shocked me. The jolt was strong enough to make the hairs on my arms stand straight up, and my entire arm jerked.

I kept my face emotionless, not even blinking. "Is that the best you've got?"

It was stupid to taunt her. Brooklyn knew how to wield her powers. Me? I had no clue what I was doing.

She released my hand, blue fire burning in her eyes. "Let's get one thing straight. This isn't just about Torent, no matter how good-looking he is. Our families, they don't mix. Isn't that right, ladies?"

I felt sorry for Leena and Cora. They both did a kind of odd shifting of their feet, but nodded their heads dutifully.

"Is this one of those, the school is only big enough for one of us deals?" I retorted, making a mental note to ask Gigi what was with the Kendall clan. Brooklyn's hatred for me went deeper than boyfriend jealousy. If I was going to survive my senior year, I would need to know what I was up against.

"Torent said you were smart," she sneered.

Torent Stark talked too much. "What is your problem with me?"

"Don't you know? Aww," she moaned like she was petting a kitten. "Did your family keep that from you as well? It must be hard living in the dark while everyone else around you laughs."

All I saw was red, a haze of it filtering over my eyes, with Brooklyn as the target. I was barely aware of the chaos whirling around me. Everything metal in the room began to tremble—weights, screws in the machines, chains hanging from the ceiling. The sounds clattered, but my focus was only on Brooklyn. I jumped off the machine and pounced on her, tackling her to the ground. The other two girls, Leena and Cora, squealed, scampering to get out of our way or risk getting hit.

"Oh, my god," I heard Beck say behind me.

No one talked bad about my family. Brooklyn could take shots at me all day, but bringing Gigi or Mom into it pushed me over the edge. I'd never been much of a fighter, but I also wasn't afraid to stand up to a mean girl.

And she fought like one too.

Grabbing a fist of my ponytail, Brooklyn yanked my head back, and the hissing pain at the hair follicles caused my arm to reach up. My elbow caught her in the jaw as I tried to loosen the hold she had on my hair.

"You white-trash waffle," she seethed, rolling her weight into me.

If I hadn't been so filled with rage, I would have laughed. *Waffle? Really?*

Brooklyn had a good ten pounds on me and managed to pin me to the stinky floor mats, a waterfall of dark hair curtaining around us. Her nails raked over my left cheek, taking a layer of my skin. I hissed.

Before I got the chance to retaliate, Ms. Collins, a PE teacher, secured her arms around Brooklyn's waist and pulled her off me.

"What is going on here?" she demanded.

I shot to my feet, but Beck grabbed me, stopping me from advancing. My breath came out in quick pants, and I touched the side of my face, knowing I was bleeding.

"You're crazy. They should have you caged, you animal," Brooklyn hurled, struggling against Ms. Collins' hold.

"Enough!" boomed Ms. Collins, the muscle along her thick neck popping out. "The two of you, principal's office. Now!" Her finger shot to the double doors of the exercise room.

My face was probably red from exertion, but I could feel it deepening. I opened my mouth to ask if Principal Friske was even in his office after school hours, but wisely snapped it shut. Why make things worse?

"Are you okay?" Beck asked, releasing me.

I stalked toward the exit doors, needing to put as much space between Brooklyn and myself as possible. "Yeah. Angry, but I'll be okay."

Beck followed, and I loved him for it. "That was the single coolest thing that has happened all year."

"I'm going to kill Torent Stark," I growled under my breath as I smoothed my crazy post-girl-fight hair. "How could he tell her about me? I confided in him."

That bastard. I had trusted Torent. Of all people, why would he tell *her* what I was?

Torent Stark was going to wish he had never met me. Demon or not, I would kick his fine ass all the way to China.

"Hey, you don't know that it was him," Beck tried to reason. "Brooklyn is evil. Who knows how many spies she has?"

"It was him. Who else could it be?" I insisted.

Beck strutted down the hall beside me in his blue-and-silver shorts and T-shirt like it was the hottest fashion trend. "Torent has a reputation, but what Brooklyn is implying is out of character, even for him. Why don't you ask him before you chop off his balls?"

I turned to look at him, a wry grin on my lips. "Where's the fun in that?"

I FOUND Torent at the shop after school. My little escapade had earned me a Saturday detention. Joy. I didn't trust myself to confront Torent at school. One visit to the principal's office in a day was my max, and I was mad enough to cause another scene.

He was wearing an old pair of jeans with grease stains that would never come out no matter how many washes it went through. It too had seen better days.

And still, he managed to make the oily getup look hot.

No. He is not hot. He is a jerk.

A distinct scent of gasoline and oil that I found intoxicating wafted in the air. He was bent under the hood of a classic car, wiggling some kind of black hose in in the engine. I stood just outside the open garage, not bothering to say his name or announce my arrival. How could I, when I couldn't take my eyes off his butt?

Focus, Mallory! I took a breath. "How could you betray me like that?" I snapped.

Torent lifted his dark head, peering over at me. For a second, it looked as if he was going to flash those deadly dimples, but when he got a look at my scowl, he obviously changed his mind. "I don't know what you think I did, crash car, but we need to talk."

"Damn straight we do. That's why I'm here," I affirmed through clenched teeth. "Brooklyn was more than happy to fill me in. Why would you tell her what I am?"

He smeared the palm of his dirty hands on the thighs of his jeans. "Calm down. There is a lot of metal in this place, and I really don't want to end up with part of an engine hitting me on the side of the head. So you're not here about the dream?" he asked.

I poked my finger into his chest, not caring if I got dirty. "Don't you dare tell me to calm down!"

"You need to lower your voice," he hissed, eyes darting over the shop. "Before someone hears you."

"Do you think I care?" Yes, I was being completely irrational and over the top. That happened when I got upset. I blamed my Irish blood.

"Mal, I didn't tell her. I didn't have to."

I stared at him unblinkingly. "What is that supposed to mean?"

Torent slipped a hand under my elbow, leading me outside. "I'm at work. I can't talk about this now," he said through his teeth.

Argh! He was so frustrating. There was nothing worse than ignoring your better judgment and then having that person disappoint you. What had I expected? He had demon blood running through his veins.

"Whatever. I should never have trusted you." I spun on my heels and stomped off to my car, slamming the door shut. Before the engine roared to life, Torent called my name, but I ignored the demon and floored the gas pedal, squealing my tires as I left the shop.

Torent Stark was an asshat of the worst kind.

I should have stuck to my plan. Go to class. Do my homework. Graduate from high school. And then get the hell out of here. My heart wouldn't be hurting as it was. The pain squeezed my chest, making it difficult to breathe. It was better this way, before my feelings got tangled.

I was kidding myself if I thought I didn't already have feelings for Torent.

It wasn't until I was halfway home that I remembered he mentioned something about a dream. I slammed on the brakes and idled in the middle of the road. Luckily, no one was behind me.

"Holy crap," I muttered. No way he could mean the same dream? Right? I was going to hyperventilate.

As PREARRANGED, Thursday after school Beck and I headed over to Sun and Moon Academy. I had two hours to kill before my supernatural evening class started.

"Do you know what we need first?" Beck asked.

I craned my neck to look left and right at the intersection before turning onto the road. "I have no idea, but I assume you're going to tell me."

"Tacos," he announced.

"I think I'm in love with you."

"That's what they all say, and then Torent Stark walks into the room."

I playfully whacked him on the arm. "Stop it. So not true."

Driving down Main Street, I whipped my car into an open spot near where the Tacos for Daze truck was parked. The smell of spices hit us as we made our way down the sidewalk.

"Did you know that the owner, Sky Spill Water, is rumored to be a troll?" Beck murmured into my ear.

"Shut up," I whispered. "A troll? You lie."

He made an X mark over his chest. "Cross my heart and hope to die."

Since school had recently ended, a line had formed. Beck and I got behind a few kids I recognized. They said hi to Beck, before returning to whatever TV show they were discussing.

"You're going to flip over Sky's tacos," Beck assured me.

Sky was wearing a bright Hawaiian-patterned shirt that was making my eyes go loopy. His long gray hair was woven into little braids, and it was all I could do to keep a straight face, thanks to Beck and his troll theory.

My eyes scanned over the menu, and I snickered. "Does he really name all his food after Grateful Dead songs?"

"See, I told you. Troll," he whispered, grinning.

Beck ordered us a couple of Mexicali Blues tacos, which we scarfed down in two minutes flat on the way back to my car.

"I think I could live on those tacos for the rest of my life," I said, climbing into the passenger seat.

"Right?" Beck agreed. "Okay, now that my stomach isn't screaming at me, let me see this ring."

I wiggled in my seat, trying to get my hand into the tiny pocket of my jeans. *Who the hell designs these? And when did pockets become so stinkin' small?* The only thing it was big enough to fit was a ring.

Beck took the little gold band, examining it under the waning sun. His eyes started to glow. "There is definitely something mystical about it. I'd be careful about wearing it until we figure out what kind of powers this trinket holds."

"That's a thing? Objects with magical powers?"

"You bet your fine ass it is. Let's go to the library and dig up some dirt." He handed me back the ring. "Best to keep it hidden for now. In the wrong hands, who knows what might happen."

A shiver rolled through me. What if something had already been unleashed?

It was a bleak thought, but I was afraid there might be a ring of truth to it.

CHAPTER 11

$\mathscr{T}$he Sun and Moon Academy library was a book nerd's dream. Rich polished wood shelves lined the walls from floor to ceiling with leather bound books just waiting to be read. Stained glass covered one wall, throwing beautiful colors over the gleaming floors. Two stories above our heads, the ceiling pitched into a dome, adorned with detailed paintings of supernatural creatures throughout the ages.

As if I had stepped onto sacred ground, a tingle of energy rushed over my skin. Silence followed as we moved into the room; the only sounds were Beck's and my footsteps clattering on the floor.

"There is a lot of history in here," Beck whispered. "If there is anything special or supernatural about that ring, it will be in here."

Inhaling the scent of paper and years of magical past, we sat huddled at a table in the corner, a stack of books Beck had collected surrounding us.

"These all have information on magical objects recorded throughout Havenwood Falls' history?" I inquired.

Beck nodded. "There are others tucked inside the Court's private stash, but they are highly guarded. You know about the town's wards, right?"

I plucked one of the books and began thumbing through the pages.

"We actually just covered it in class last week." There were wards that prevented magic at the schools and wards that protected the town itself—like the memory ward that kept Havenwood Falls a secret.

"It's possible this ring has a charm on it. The question is what kind of spell?"

My eyes roamed over the page. "And you think the answer lies in one of these books?"

"Maybe."

I sighed. "It will take all night to get through them all. I have class in an hour and a half."

"How bad do you want to know what the deal is with the ring?" he challenged.

Flashes of Torent and the too-hot-to-handle visions flipped through my memory. "This better not earn me another detention," I grumbled.

Beck gave me a wicked smile. "The image of you tackling Brooklyn is going to stay with me for the rest of my life."

I tossed him a book. "Get to work."

For the next hour, we poured over books older than dirt. If I hadn't been on a mission, the information in some of them would have made great reading. I had so much yet to learn about supernaturals, it almost seemed daunting.

I was beginning to think this was useless. What if the ring didn't have any spell? What if it was just a ring? Nothing more than a pretty bauble a woman lost in the lake? My foot started tapping under the table in restlessness. A low buzzing vibrated in my ears, not pesky like a mosquito, but a gentle hum. The hairs on my arms stood up, but I continued to scour through the books, not giving it a second thought.

I could sense my irritation increasing, but didn't think anything of it until something tiny hit me on the forehead. I jerked. What the—

A silver paperclip had fallen onto my book. Was someone throwing things at me? I couldn't picture the elderly woman behind the desk starting paperclip wars with us. No sooner had the thought flittered through my mind, I was hit with a second paperclip in the arm.

Beck caught the next one in his hand as his eyes shifted to mine. "You need to chill out before we end up with a collection of paperclips stuck to us. What have you learned about your ability?"

Was I doing this?

When it was brought to my attention, I became aware of the hum of energy swimming in my veins.

"Holy crap. Sorry. I'm still figuring this metal thing out." I had a revelation about my powers. Without proper training, I could be dangerous. Paperclips weren't a big deal, but knives, scissors, basically anything metal would be problems I didn't want.

"You're not the first to lose control. It happens to all of us. I once howled at the moon during soccer practice. My dad never pushed the whole sports thing again."

"Ugh. Some days I wish I had never gone into the lake."

"It's your destiny, Mal. I don't think there is much you could have done to avoid it. Fate has a way of catching up to us."

"When did you know what you were?"

"Always. But I grew up here. There are things all locals know, including to keep their distance from Peacock Lake. The waters are poisonous to humans and even some supes. It's your affinity to water that calls you to the lake. The ring didn't just fall off of anyone. Whoever lost it, they were definitely one of us, maybe even a nymph."

Like Mom or Gigi.

Food for thought, not that I needed more to think about. I grabbed another book from the stack, returning to the search for information. It seemed hopeless and a waste of time. We weren't going to find anything in this—

"Holy wereballs," Beck announced in a voice louder than a whisper. "I think I found something. Let me see the ring."

"Ssshh!" came a hissing from the little librarian.

Beck ignored her while I dug into my pocket, producing the inscribed gold band.

"This is it." He pointed to a picture in the book spread out in front of him. I craned my neck over the table as he began reading from the book. "The Teardrop of Desire." He glanced up, capturing my gaze, his eyes sparkling. "Tell me you love me."

"Beck, you're a freaking genius. I love you."

His eyes skimmed over the text below the picture. He swallowed, and I didn't like the serious frown that formed on his lips. "This is bad."

"What?" I shrieked in as quiet a voice as I could manage.

He lifted his head. "Torent was there with you when you found the ring?"

"Yeah, so?"

"Well, according to the legend, the Teardrop of Desire is one link to a magical chain—the Elan Chain. The rings were split up and divided. A witch by the name of Antanasia Gabor was given the Teardrop of Desire by her fiancé. No one knows how it came to be in his possession, but his desire for greed and power was greater than his love for Antanasia. The night before their wedding, he married another in secret, an heiress with a throne, giving Antanasia's fiancé all that he desired. Heartbroken, the witch cast a spell on the ring, offering it to the new bride as a gift. It is said the ring gives the wearer what their heart desires most, no matter how pure or dark, and by any means necessary."

Silenced followed as we absorbed what Beck had just read out loud. I didn't know what I was feeling.

"So, Mal, what do you desire?" He was half joking, but neither of us could deny the ominous undertones in the curse of the ring.

"I don't know . . . that I get out of this town and go to college."

Beck made a snoring noise and pretended to nod off.

I gave his shoulder a nudge. "Funny."

"That can't be what you desire most. What was the first thing you thought of when finding it?" he asked, trying a different route.

I thought back to the lake and the hot vision I'd had when Torent had pulled me out of the water.

"Crap," I muttered. My deepest, darkest desire was to have smoldering sex with Torent.

"Oh, I'm going to like this, aren't I?"

"Beck!" I hissed. "This is serious."

"Torent was with you. There isn't a girl in Havenwood Falls that wouldn't have immediately desired that piece of man-flesh."

"Oh, my god," I groaned, laying my head on the table. "This can't be happening." I quickly lifted my face and looked at Beck. "How do I reverse it or whatever?"

His eyes scanned the rest of the page. "It doesn't say, but it does note that the curse only works when the ring is worn."

Only me. A string of colorful f-bombs rolled off my lips.

I MANAGED to avoid Torent for the rest of the week. One, I was still miffed at the demon. And two, since I unearthed the curse on the ring, I thought it was best I didn't tempt myself. If these feelings I had for Torent weren't real, if they were because of the ring, it would be better if I didn't wear the thing.

The idea of magic dictating my feelings was invasive. Since I found the origin of the ring, I questioned everything, every moment Torent and I had ever shared. Had any of it been real? My night classes and catching up in school helped keep my mind off him.

I walked into Coffee Haven with the agenda of studying and drinking enough lattes to have me peeing coffee for a week. The blueberry scone I ordered was just an added bonus. To die for. Now I understood what everyone at school raved about.

Sunlight streamed through the window, warming my cheeks as I sipped on my coffee, my calculus textbook sprawled out on the table. I attacked the assignment, fueled by sugar and caffeine.

Halfway into my homework, a dark shadow fell over my notebook. It only took the tingles radiating down my neck to tell me who it was. I didn't bother to look up. "What do you want?"

"Can we talk?" asked a low and husky voice.

My pencil etched a solid black line under problem number thirty-five. "No."

"Mal, you're being unreasonable," he growled in a texture my ears found sexy.

I *was* being unreasonable, but I didn't care. I sighed and finally glanced up, meeting Torent's vibrant gaze. "You betrayed me, or have you so quickly forgotten?"

His eyes held mine with an expression I couldn't decipher. "I did not. I wouldn't do that."

"Says the demon."

"Half demon," he corrected. The chair across from me scooted over the floor and was filled with his tall form as he took the liberty of sitting down.

"That seat's taken," I said, tapping the end of my pencil on the notebook.

His elbows leaned on the table. "Too bad. You're going to listen to what I have to say. Brooklyn is a water nymph like you."

The air halted in my chest.

"She's what?" I shrieked. Of all the things she could be, never once had nymph crossed my mind. I had figured vampire or witch, something hostile.

He leaned over the table with such intensity in his eyes. "Brooklyn, Leena, and Cora, they're all nymphs. Brooklyn has an affinity for water, like you, but Leena's is forests and Cora's is meadows."

I searched his face, sinking into the chair. "And you didn't think I should know this? God, I feel so stupid. She told me you went to see her after you dropped me off."

"She wasn't lying," he mumbled.

"Oh." I didn't know what to say. My heart had just dropped out of my chest.

"It's not what you think," he quickly added.

"And how would you know what I'm thinking?" I fired back.

"Your mind is always going, but it's your face that gives it away. I meant what I said about things between Brooklyn and me being over. I went there to tell her just that." I don't know how or when, but his fingers had found mine on the table. The pad of his thumb was making lazy circles over my hand as if he was compelled to touch me.

I pulled my hand away from his, frowning. "I don't think she took it well."

Something flickered over his face. Irritation? "Brooklyn never does. One of the many reasons we didn't work out."

I averted my gaze down to my notebook for fear of doing something stupid. I had deliberately left the ring at home, but even without the cursed piece of jewelry, I still felt an insurmountable pull to Torent. My body naturally wanted to sway toward him. My fingers itched to touch his face. And the things my lips wanted to do were downright sinful. *Focus, Mal. What had he said? Right, Brooklyn. Water nymph.*

"Wow. I can't believe we're the same species. That doesn't mean we're related, does it? Like third cousins twice removed or some shit?"

"I don't think so. Brooklyn is a descendant of the goddess Aphrodite."

I choked. She would have the DNA of love and beauty. Just another reason to hate her. At least we had different bloodlines. Being related to her would have been a living nightmare. "Does she know you're telling me this?"

He shrugged. "Everyone in the supe world knows. Brooklyn hasn't exactly kept who she is a secret. Just the opposite. She thrives on the attention."

Very true. "What abilities does she have?"

"A wicked shock."

That I could attest to.

"Brooklyn siphons energy from around her. Electricity is readily available, making it easy for her to tap into," he explained.

Since Torent was being so forthcoming, I pushed on.

"Do you know what happened between our families?" I asked.

He didn't immediately answer, appearing to have some sort of internal debate with himself. "Bits and pieces. Something happened between your parents and Brooklyn's before you were born. I don't know what, but it drove a wedge between your families. Your mom used to be best friends with Brooklyn's."

"Really?" It was hard for me to picture my mom being friends with anyone who resembled Brooklyn, especially if she was anything like her daughter.

"I could press her for more details if you think it's important," he added, and my heart fluttered. He had a way of making me feel like he would do anything for me.

I cursed the damn ring. Something told me having that kind of loyalty from Torent would inspire deep emotions. "Because you want an excuse to see her or you want to help me?"

His hand flew to his chest in a wounded gesture. "Ouch. That stung. I'm not an asshole all the time, crash car."

"I don't want to tip her off that I'm digging into our families' past. I'll see what I can find out from Gigi." I absently touched my finger where the band would have been, had I worn it.

His eyes were drawn to the motion, glancing at my hand. "You're not wearing the ring, the one you found at the lake that day."

I shook my head. "No."

Did I tell him what Beck and I had discovered?

He stretched his hand across the table but stopped himself before he touched mine. "I'm good at detecting evil things—demon senses. There is something about that ring that gives me bad vibes."

He must have changed his mind about not touching me. As his eyes moved upward to my face, I felt drawn to him. The pad of his thumb had returned to make lazy circles over my hand, and I leaned forward, unable to help myself.

"We need to talk, but not here. Can you meet me later?" I whispered, making a rash decision to tell him everything.

His lips parted as he leaned forward, bringing our faces close together. "Is this some kind of ploy to get me alone?"

"Yes and no."

"Okay," he agreed, a smirk teasing his lips.

"Tonight."

Mischief flared in his eyes. "I'll pick you up."

I took an unsteady breath. It was settled. I was doing the very thing I told myself I wouldn't do—let my heart rule my life.

Why was it so hard to say no to Torent? I wanted to blame the ring, but was it really a curse that was making me think about the demon every waking moment?

CHAPTER 12

I couldn't believe I was sneaking out to see a boy. A demon, no less! Mom would be so proud.

As the rest of the house slept, I tiptoed around my room, cursing the old floorboards. Through the sheer curtains on the window, a shimmer of moonlight cast ghostly dancing shadows.

I spent way too much time on my appearance. My floor looked like a hurricane of clothes had just blown through. Nothing was ever where it was supposed to be when I needed it, and that included my really good bra, the one that made me actually look like I had boobs.

Torent would be here in fifteen minutes, and I was still running around half naked. No big deal. All I had to do was find those jeans, the ones that made my butt look fantastic.

I stared at my room and declared it a hopeless war zone. Grabbing the first pair I could find, I lay on my bed and wiggled into them. Sitting in front of the vanity, I checked my hair one last time, studying the waves of blond hair framing my face. I swiftly reapplied my mascara and slapped on some lip gloss. Without giving my appearance another thought, I grabbed my phone off the bed, shoved it into the back pocket of my jeans, and snatched the ring from inside the drawer.

Cracking the bedroom door, I peeked down the hall and took a breath. The first few steps I took at turtle speed, deathly afraid the floor would groan under my weight, but the suspense of possibly getting caught got to me, and I raced the remainder of the way downstairs. Of course, the front door creaked like an old woman, but I barreled through, stepping outside.

Torent's Jeep was idling in the driveway, and I didn't have to see inside the car to know he was laughing at me.

I padded across the lawn, and before I got to the car, Torent was waiting with the door open.

"Is it normal for demons to have manners?" I asked, eyeing him.

He chuckled. "I was raised by a demon, but I also had a mother who made damn sure I wasn't a jerk all the time."

I got comfortable inside the Jeep as I waited for him to walk around the car. I told myself not to breathe in the pine and mint scent that was all Torent, but my senses seemed to not listen to my brain. I wanted to bottle the smell and use it as a pillow spray.

He put one hand on the steering wheel and the other on the shifter. "Where to, crash car?"

I blinked, still reeling from the intoxicating aroma of his car. "Anywhere but here."

"Buckle up. Let's see if we can get lost in the mountains."

That was not what I had in mind.

"I'm here to talk, not make out," I stated, making my intention clear.

He backed the car out with a grin on his face that said he didn't believe a word of it. "Who says we can't do both?"

"Torent," I groaned. *Goddess Styx, give me strength.*

"You know, that might be the first time you've said my name. I like it."

"Don't get used to it. I'm thinking jackass suits you better."

His deep laugh filled the Jeep.

We drove away from the center of town to where the road wound upward. The landscape might have been breathtaking, but I couldn't take my eyes off Torent. I really needed to get rid of this ring.

He parked the Jeep, and I struggled for some way to start this

85

conversation. How did I tell a guy he might not really have feelings for me?

"It's so beautiful at night," I murmured, gazing at the bright lights dotting the town below. That was lame.

In the dark, I felt Torent's fingers graze the side of my face.

"Yes, you are," he whispered.

Don't look at him. Don't do it. Too late. My eyes were already moving through the darkness to search out his. "That was super cheesy."

"Doesn't make it any less true." His voice was gruff and sexy, all the things I didn't want him to be. An electric moment sparked between us, and I was stunned by the intensity.

My cheeks flushed, and I was grateful for the cover of night to disguise the heightened color. Drawing my legs up on the seat, I leaned onto the center console. The movement settled me closer to Torent.

Don't kiss him. It's the ring. Remember the ring? It's the whole reason you're alone with Torent Stark!

My brain was such a buzzkill. The only thing I wanted right then was Torent's lips on mine. There would be time to discuss the ring later, after I tasted him, ripped his clothes off, and devoured him.

He leaned near my ear and whispered, "Mallory."

The sound of my name on his lips created tiny coils in the pit of my belly. My tongue darted out, wetting my lips. A shiver rolled through him, and I watched in awe as the purple in his irises melded to liquid gold—his demon eyes.

"Can you control the changing of your eyes?" I asked, completely entranced by them.

"Most of the time, but there are moments they shift of their own accord. Like now." His lips brushed over mine.

I wasn't prepared for the feelings that rocked through me from just a light kiss. My fingers bunched the material of his shirt. "Just. One. Kiss."

His lips curved against mine. "If you say so."

Then he was kissing me, and my brain turned to gooey mush.

I had no self-control when it came to Torent, and I wasn't sure I could keep blaming the ring. Kissing him was the last thing I should be doing, but I didn't want to fight what he made me feel, not when my body was humming.

He tilted his head to the side, putting the slightest pressure on my lips with his tongue. I knew what he wanted. Parting my lips, I sighed at the first taste of him inside my mouth.

Something primitive rose up within me, and if I wasn't careful, this kiss would spiral to the point of no return. I hadn't much thought about the guy I would lose my V-card to, but Torent was as damn good as any.

No!

Your first time is not going to be inside his Jeep. Not happening.

It was far too cliché.

I pushed my hand at his chest, fighting the urge to pull him across the seat. "No more kissing."

"Do you really want me to stop?" he asked, his gold eyes burning bright while his lips cruised along my jaw and to the side of my neck, where the vein pulsed wildly.

"No . . . yes," I corrected and sat back in my seat, giving myself a moment of clarity, but it was short-lived when a burst of swirling colors lit up the Jeep.

"It's amazing, isn't it?" he murmured, twisting our fingers together as the light whirled in the dark.

"That's not the point."

"So tell me, crash car, what is the point then?"

"This." I pulled out the ring. I shouldn't have been astonished to see that the center stone was glowing like fire. It washed both our faces in a radiant red.

"You still have that thing?" His face scrunched up, and he backed away from the ring, leaning against the door.

"Do you know what it is?" I asked, seeing his reaction. It was clear Torent didn't get lovey vibes from the cursed stone.

"It has an aura of dark magic, that much I can tell you. I don't think it is safe for you to have in your possession."

"Beck and I did some research."

"The wolf?"

I nodded. I knew they didn't run in the same circles, but Torent had to have known how close Beck and I had grown. I gave him the rundown of what Beck and I had discovered.

"We need to turn this over to the Court," Torent said, after I finished spilling the details on the ring. "A relic with that much power shouldn't be floating around Havenwood Falls. In the wrong hands, it could be catastrophic."

I agreed.

"Will you take it?" I asked, holding out the ring for him to grab. I didn't trust anyone else.

Torent shook his head as something flickered in his gold eyes. Temptation? "I don't dare touch it. The last thing you want to do is give a demon something that powerful. It would be dangerous for everyone. I won't tempt myself, but I will take you to the Court to turn it over."

Good enough. So I was stuck with it until then. What could go wrong? Famous last words. "Okay. Monday after school?"

He stared at my hand. "Keep it hidden until then."

Because I could see that the ring was making him uncomfortable, I slipped the little band back into my pocket.

"Do you think it's possible that the ring is messing with my emotions?" I asked, chewing on my lower lip. The question made me feel vulnerable.

Torent peered over at me through thick lashes. "Are you trying to blame the ring because you can't keep your hands off me?"

I snorted. "No, that is not what I'm saying. Please. You're not that irresistible."

A sardonic twist curled his lips, and I knew I was going to regret baiting him as my belly fluttered. "Would you like to test that theory?"

Crossing my arms, I said, "I think you should take me home."

Torent had a different idea. "I think we should go skinny dipping in the falls."

"Are you insane? Do you have any idea how cold the water must be?"

"Heat—or cold—is not really a problem for me—demon blood," he answered my question. "And I'm betting your affinity for water allows you to withstand any temperature."

He might be right, but no way was I swimming naked with Torent Stark.

No freaking way!

He started to take his shirt off and . . .

CHAPTER 13

orent was shirtless. Every sensible thought failed me as I felt my resolve weakening. My skin was on fire. Nothing in the world sounded more refreshing than a dip in the water. It was the only way to cool the inferno that had started to spread through my veins.

"Put your shirt back on," I demanded in the weakest voice ever.

Opening his car door, he stepped out, spreading his arms open. "Welcome to the falls, crash car."

"Torent," I growled. "Get back in the car."

His fingers were at the button on his pants. He flipped it through the loop and was about to start on the zipper. "I swear I'm not a bad influence. Come on. Let's go swimming. The water is calling your name."

The thing was, if I closed my eyes, I probably would hear the gentle song, lulling me into the waters. I'd heard the call my whole life. There was nowhere I felt more at home than submerged underwater.

"I hate you," I grumbled. Ignoring his chuckle, I pressed the door handle and let myself out of the Jeep. He had already moved down toward the water, and I followed onto the rocky clearing and nearly sighed. "It's amazing."

The falls might have been prettier under moonlight with a million stars twinkling over our heads. There it was in the center of my chest

—that gentle tug, nudging me closer to the water. It grew with each step I took, and I didn't pause until I reached the edge.

Crouching down, I dipped my hand into the water. Tingles skipped over my skin like little beads of electricity.

"What are you waiting for?"

I flipped my gaze over my shoulder, and I probably should have steadied myself first, but I honestly hadn't expected to see a nearly naked Torent standing behind me.

Sweet baby Jesus.

He could have at least warned me. Abs alert. It wasn't like I'd never seen a guy in his boxers. I had Netflix, for goddess's sake. This shouldn't be a big deal.

But I was wrong. Dead wrong.

Torent had an athletic build, not overly muscular, but he definitely kept in shape. It didn't look like he had an ounce of fat on him. I wasn't sure how long I stood gawking, but my cheeks grew warm when I finally became aware.

His gold eyes were glowing eerily in the dark. "Don't get shy on me now, crash car."

As he moved backward into the water, his eyes never left mine.

I needed a moment to get a grip. *What is the big deal? How many times have you worn a bathing suit in front of guys? Why is my bra and undies any different? It isn't.* Except they were lacy, black, and thinner, my mind pointed out.

Lifting my chin, I straightened up and tugged my shirt slowly over my head. A gust of brisk wind blew over my skin, making my nipples pucker. I refused to cross my arms over my chest, regardless of how much I wanted to.

Aware of his eyes watching my every move, a mixture of embarrassment and sexiness danced around inside me. It was hard to decide which emotion was winning.

Mallory.

The water called me, and my attention was diverted. I no longer felt awkward, only a longing I couldn't suppress. Unsnapping the button on my jeans, I wiggled out of them and waded my feet into the water.

Mallory.

The voices called again. Not one, but many, all singing my name like a thousand angels.

I closed my eyes as a surge of power rose from the tips of my toes to the crown of my head, and I stepped deeper into the water. It was indescribable, what I was feeling, as if I could sense every molecule in the water.

"What am I going to do about you?" Torent had lost his smile and was staring at me with a piercing gaze that reached my core.

The water was neither warm nor cold as it glided over my skin. I stumbled for something snarky to say, but the truth was, I didn't know what to do about him either. "It looks like we're in the same predicament."

He went under, and I watched his dark form swim, resurfacing in front of me. Water dripped over his face, sticking to his long lashes. "What are we going to do about it?"

"Not what you're thinking."

"And how do you know what's going on inside my head?"

I dipped my shoulders into the water, letting the waves produced by the falls take me closer to Torent. The ends of my hair haloed around me. "Because you're a guy, and you've got that look in your eyes."

He grabbed my hand, and I let out a little squeal of surprise. He pulled me with him to the center of the pool, my feet treading water as I eyed him.

"What look?" he asked, knowing damn well what I was talking about.

A wave came out of nowhere, pushing me into Torent's arms, and I began to wonder if the water was conspiring against me. I had no other explanation for the sudden gust of water strong enough to throw me off balance. Were my goddess ancestors trying to tell me something?

My hands came up to land on his shoulders lest I risk going under. "Trouble," I whispered.

A long moment passed. His chest rose against mine, sparking almost electric sensations inside me, and when his fingers brushed a piece of hair off my face, that feeling tripled. My power seemed to want to answer his. I leaned my head back, and my breath caught. Above our heads, green, purple, and aqua lights swirled. The aurora borealis we created was floating over the falls.

I thought the view had been breathtaking before. Now, it was like I was living in a fantasy.

The light show above our heads brightened in color.

"A little trouble is good," he murmured.

"Only a demon would say that."

The corner of his lips twitched as his hands roamed to my hips, keeping me from drifting away. In the water, he was no challenge for me. If I had wanted to escape, nothing he could have done would have stopped me. This was my domain. And he knew it.

His lips touched mine, and I breathed in the scent of the falls mixed with Torent's. One of my hands looped around his neck, and the other traced along his jawline, feeling the tiny stubbles of facial hair. My lips parted, inviting him to take so much more, and he responded with a hunger to match mine.

This was dangerous.

Alone.

So few clothes.

And a guy who had the ability to consume me with just a kiss.

Screw it.

I was young.

The moon was full.

And I only lived once.

Wrapping my legs around his waist, I twirled my tongue around the metal stud pierced in his as I captured his moan. His fingers strayed from my hips to cup my backside.

I'd kissed other guys before, but nothing compared to locking lips with Torent. It was like coming home, and what he could evoke inside me was frightening.

Torent broke off the kiss suddenly with a look of murder in his expression. It stunned me at first, before I realized something was wrong. The muscles in his body tightened while he kept me pressed against him.

Over the crash of the falls drifted what I could have sworn were voices and laughter. It couldn't be, not this late, right?

Wrong.

"We're not alone," Torent said, the deep gravel in his voice menacing. "Not that I'm surprised."

Should I be concerned?

His body language made it seem as if something not good might be coming this way.

And he was right.

"Looks like we're late to the party." The intruder's voice made me cringe.

Fuck. Brooklyn.

She sure knew how to ruin a good night.

And the queen bee wasn't alone. She never was, though. A group of kids trotted down the trail behind her, including her two little minions, Cora and Leena.

"What are you doing here?" Torent demanded.

"Just having a little fun, same as you, but we brought party favors." Brooklyn held up two bottles of wine, which was followed by a few chuckles and snickers. "Did we interrupt something?"

I wanted to claw her pretty blue eyes out. She knew darn well she had.

"We were just leaving," Torent said with a frown. He moved away from me, but laced our fingers together and pulled me toward the shore. Under the water, a glow of lights danced. I unwound our hands quickly to avoid any unwanted attention.

"Don't be a party pooper," Brooklyn pouted from the edge of the water. "You've never skipped out on a chance to have fun before."

I tried not to think about how little clothes I had on as we emerged out of the lake, but the whistles from the boys from school didn't help. Torent's eyes began to flash in flecks of gold. I laid a hand on his forearm.

"Let's just go, okay?" There was no need for a fight to break out.

I wasn't sure he heard me, his eyes becoming more gold than purple, but then he turned away from the small group, grabbing his stuff.

I scooped my shirt off the ground and whipped it over my head, not caring that I was soaking wet. Damp clothes were the least of my problems. I wiggled into my jeans, grabbed my shoes, and stormed my way to the car.

"You can be such a witch," I heard Torent growl to Brooklyn as I climbed up the path.

"Coming from you, I'll take that as a compliment," Brooklyn retorted, her voice snapping.

"Are you okay?" Torent asked, sliding into the driver's seat, his keys jingling in his hand.

I nodded. "I'm fine. Just take me home."

Without another word, he turned they key in the ignition and the engine ripped to life. I sat back in the seat, staring up at the moon. I shouldn't let Brooklyn get to me, but she made it so easy to hate her.

I closed my eyes, and when I opened them again, Torent was rolling down my driveway with his lights off. He shifted the Jeep into park. "I'm sorry about Brooklyn."

"You don't need to apologize for her."

"Probably not, but she has a way making a nuisance of herself."

"Thanks for the ride and the . . . interesting night." I reached for the door handle.

His lips curled, and I found that even in my state of irritation, I wanted to brush the lock of hair off his forehead. "Anytime, crash car. Don't forget the ring. Monday after school?"

The ring.

I reached into my pocket to make sure it was still safely tucked inside my jeans. The first string of panic descended when I found both my pockets empty.

No. No. No.

This can't be happening.

Turning in the seat, I combed the leather, before moving to the floor, tearing the inside of Torent's Jeep apart.

Holy crap.

It was gone.

"What are you doing?" Torent's husky voice sounded in the dark. He was watching me with a curious expression.

I spun. "The ring. It's gone," I hissed, panic leaking into my tone.

His eyes narrowed. "What do you mean gone?"

"Gone. As in I don't have it anymore. Do you need me to spell it out for you? G-O-N—"

"You made your point. When was the last time you remember having it?"

"Before you got the bright idea to go swimming at the falls."

Torent's eyes held mine, and we came to the same conclusion.

"Brooklyn!" we both roared in unison.

He forked a hand through his still damp hair. "I'll talk to her."

My anxiety reached new levels. "Is that safe? Who the hell knows what she is capable of, with something like that in her possession?"

"Are you worried about me?"

"I'm concerned about everyone in this town." Myself included. Brooklyn and I had no love lost between us, and with our families' bad blood, I didn't doubt I was one of her prime targets.

I shuddered to think what Brooklyn desired most.

"First we need to make sure she has the ring. I'll go back and check the falls to be safe."

Nodding, I wrung my hands together in my lap. We both knew it would be wasted effort. The ring hadn't grown legs and walked away. His devious ex had swiped it from me.

"Don't worry. We'll find it."

How was he not freaking out? We could have potentially unleashed a psychopath into Havenwood Falls. If Gigi or Mom found out . . .

I was so dead.

CHAPTER 14

*H*alloween had barfed all over the halls of Havenwood Falls High. They seemed to take the spooky holiday seriously. Orange, purple, and black balloons arched around the doorways. The halls were decorated in webs, spiders dangling over our heads. It was kind of cute and made me miss trick-or-treating as a kid. Addison and I had lived only a block away from each other. We strategically mapped our neighborhood to maximize our candy haul, and there would always be a sleepover afterward, staying up late, popcorn, and a scary movie.

I missed her—missed my old life. No demons. No nymphs. No evil ring.

Growing up sucked.

"Are you going to the Haunting on Main Street Wednesday night?" Beck asked. He was sitting beside me in study hall.

Wednesday was Halloween and apparently was a big deal around here.

"Should I be?" I couldn't think about tomorrow, let alone what I would be doing Wednesday night, not with the ring still missing.

"Yes," he hissed back, rubbing at his temples.

"Is you-know-who going to be there?" The last person in the world

I wanted to see was Brooklyn, and if there was a party, I doubted she was far behind.

"Would you believe me if I said no?"

I went back to doodling in my notebook. "I'm busy."

Beck looped his arm through mine, causing my pen to dart across the page. "I'm not taking no for an answer. I need a sidekick, and girl, you're it."

"Are you going to wolf out on me?" I whispered.

He grinned. "Is it a full moon? I can never remember."

You'd think that was something a shifter would remember. "Does this require me to dress up?"

His eyes glanced at my notebook, looking at the hearts scribbled over the paper. "Only if you don't want to be lame."

I groaned.

"Come on, it will be a blast. You can't miss your first Halloween here. We can go shopping after school at Callie's and pick out costumes."

"Fine." I sighed. "But I can't go today." He seemed so excited. How could I disappoint him, regardless that I didn't feel much in the party mood?

"And why is that? No night classes, so a date with Havenwood Falls High's resident cutie then?"

"Hardly." My eyes swept the room before I lowered my voice. "Brooklyn stole the ring."

"She what!" he shouted, earning him a scowl from Mr. Arroyo.

Our study hall teacher was a science nerd. His voice was a tad too high, and he looked like he could use a protein shake with a good dose of vitamin E. Damn. Maybe he was a vampire—a gangly, clumsy one at that.

"Is there a problem, Mr. Winslow?" he asked, raising a brow over his wire-rimmed glasses.

Beck tilted his head to the side. "Depends if boredom is a crime."

"Keep it down. Or I'll be forced to separate you from Ms. Dorian."

"Got it, chief." Beck pretended to open his textbook. "Why am I just now hearing about this? What happened?" he murmured.

I tapped my pen against my cheek. "It's a long story, but the short version is, I snuck out to see Torent over the weekend to tell him what we found out about the ring. One thing led to another, and we ended up swimming in the falls when Brooklyn pickpocketed me."

"Wait. Just. A. Second. Let's back it up to the part where you got naked with Torent freaking Stark."

I rolled my eyes. "I did not get naked with Torent. I was wearing a bra and panties."

He shuddered. "Don't say that word. It gives me the willies."

"Panties," I echoed, because seeing him squirm was too much fun for me to let it go.

He made a disgusted face. "I thought we were friends."

I chuckled.

"What are we going to do now that she has the Teardrop of Desire?" he asked, as if I had all the answers.

"Torent's going to see if he can get it from her. I'm meeting him after school."

Beck scowled. "That sounds like a really bad idea. I'm coming with you."

My head shook. "I don't want to get you mixed up in this. I can't help but shake this feeling something bad is going to happen if I don't find it."

"Yeah, Brooklyn is going to read us all our last rites and then shock us to death."

I mulled over the image he created, and the scary part was, I could see it unfold. "I wish I had never found it."

A body slid into the seat next to mine, and I could tell from the tingles racing down my spine and the glint of excitement in Beck's eyes, Torent had occupied the seat beside me. I don't know how he got away with coming into a class and no one saying anything. I turned to look at him, but found that his violet gaze slid past me to Beck. "Give us a minute?"

I put a hand on Beck's arm.

"It's okay. He knows. I thought we were meeting after school, not during classes," I rumbled as quietly as I could at Torent.

But then he had to go and flash me a pair of dimples that would make a nun's knees weak. "I got impatient. I needed to see you."

My heart galloped in my chest. Why did every word out of his mouth have to induce such strong feelings inside me? With the ring gone, I had assumed this intensity would fade between us. That didn't seem to be the case. "Did you find it?"

If he thought about objecting to Beck being in on our little powwow, he must have changed his mind. "It wasn't at the falls. Someone definitely picked it up."

"You mean she stole it from me. Does she have it?"

"She said she'd never seen a ring."

I snorted. "You don't believe her, do you?"

"I've known Brooklyn my whole life, and I know when she is hiding something. She is definitely up to something."

"Shit."

Torent leaned an elbow on the desk.

"How much did you tell him?" he asked, talking about Beck.

I blinked. "Everything."

Torent leaned in so we shared the same air.

"Everything?" he repeated in a deep voice that oozed sensuality. His gaze held me hostage.

Heat spread over my cheeks as his scent teased me. I wanted to be anywhere but in a classroom. The back of his car. The janitor's closet. Under the bleachers. Dear God, I needed to get myself under control.

Beck took his notebook, fanning himself, and cooed, "It's getting hot in here."

I kicked him under the table as Torent laughed. "What are we going to do? We're not going to get Brooklyn to just hand it over."

It would mean she would have to admit what she had done. And that was very, very unlikely.

"There's a Halloween party on Wednesday night. Go with me?"

"What does that have to do with—"

Now it was Beck's turn to kick me.

I glared at him.

"You'd better say yes," Beck hissed between his teeth. "And I want details."

"Two against one." Torent grinned. "Looks like I win. I'll pick you up at seven. And, crash car, don't forget your mask. We're going to test your inner bad with a bit of B and E."

"Is that some kind of kinky supernatural sex thing, because I think I'll pass."

Both Beck and Torent snickered.

"Mal, I love you," Beck said. "I'll make sure she is properly outfitted on one condition. You swear to me you'll keep her safe."

My eyes bounced between them. "Why do I need his protection?"

They both ignored me. "You have my word. No harm will come to her. We need to get the ring back and turn it over to the Court. I don't think I need to tell you what an object like that can do in the wrong hands?"

And Brooklyn definitely qualified as the wrong hands.

"Will someone tell me what a B and E is?" My voice had grown with mounting irritation, causing a few heads to turn in our direction.

Torent pressed his finger to my lips. He shook his head as his mouth curved in amusement. "Just be ready at seven."

Don't do it, Mallory. Don't give into him.

My eyes snapped downward and I remained silent, studying my open textbook as if it was an advanced reader copy of the next J.K. Rowling book. "Fine. But this better not earn me another detention."

He leaned over and whispered in my ear, "Live a little." The feel of his warm breath on my newly inked ear sent tingles prancing through me.

What was he doing to me?

Screwing up my entire life plan, that's what, and I didn't have the ring to blame.

"THERE IS ONLY one place in Havenwood Falls that has what we're looking for. Callie's Consignments." Beck and I were strolling down Main Street with iced coffees in hand.

I took a sip from my straw and nearly moaned. Coffee Haven was godly. "I'll take your word for it."

We walked next door to the quaint little boutique owned by Callie Montgomery. According to Beck, she was a supe. "Don't tell me you're one of those people who hate Halloween?"

The door chimed as we walked inside.

"Actually, I love it. I've just been so preoccupied, I forgot about it."

Beck gasped. "Be careful what you say."

I'd spent so much time dwelling on the ring, battling my feelings for Torent, and dealing with being a nymph, I barely gave more than a passing thought to the numerous other supernaturals in this town.

Take the cute gypsy-demon who owned this shop. Callie looked like she could be a cover model for Free People. Her smile reached her hazel eyes as she greeted Beck and me. You would never know by looking at her that she was anything but human.

We perused the racks, Beck pulling out amazing vintage finds.

"You would look killer in this. I bet Torent would love it," Beck sang, a sparkle in his eyes.

I wrinkled my nose, eyeing the black stretchy material. "No way am I wearing that."

"I don't see why not. It's sexy and perfect for a night of espionage."

"Cat Woman?" The black bodysuit was shiny and looked big enough to only fit one of my thighs. It would leave nothing to the imagination, hugging every curve in my body.

"Exactly. We can get you a tail and cat ears."

I leveled him with a stare.

One side of his lips curled up as he held up the black bodysuit.

"I bet Brooklyn would wear it," he said, dangling it in the air.

I snorted. "My point."

His shoulders sagged, and he turned on the puppy eyes. "Indulge me and at least try it on?" He held out the outfit.

"Augh, if it gets you off my back, fine." I reluctantly took the hanger and marched myself to the back of the shop, all the while grumbling under my breath. What I wanted to wear was a reaper cape to go with my sullen mood lately.

Maybe it was the loss of the ring or not knowing when Brooklyn would strike, but I hadn't felt like myself the past few days, and it was starting to wear on me.

I wasn't in a shopping mood, and I knew Beck only had the best intentions, but I hardly doubted me flaunting my curves would help me. I felt a sense of responsibility to keep the ring from causing chaos. It was my fault the ring was floating around town. If I had never gone into the water, it would still be sitting at the bottom of Peacock Lake.

While my head was whirling with guilt and uncertainty, I stripped down and shimmied into the bodysuit, swearing and grumbling every inch of the way. I turned and studied my reflection in the full-length mirror.

Holy crap.

Is that me?

When did I get hips?

I twisted from side to side, watching the fabric move with my body. It clung to my hips like a second skin. Running my hands over my thighs, I had to give it to Beck. He did have a point. I felt sexy . . . and powerful.

Maybe a little too much.

A gush of energy soared up inside me, and there was nothing I could do to stop it or the stray pins on the floor from flying at me like I was a giant magnet. Three tiny needles embedded themselves into my arm.

"Ouch!" I shrieked, feeling like a human pin cushion.

Beck whipped back the curtain. "What happened?"

I was plucking out one of the pins when he burst in, startling me, and I stabbed the pad of my index finger.

"I poked myself with a needle." I sucked on the end of my finger, drawing in the blood from the tiny pinprick.

"Do I even want to know how?"

"Stupid nymph powers," I mumbled, pulling out the other two pins.

"How's that going by the way? Not good I take it?"

"It feels as if I'm never going to get the hang of my powers." My Awakening Lab night class was supposed to help me hone my abilities, but I was the class klutz. My powers never did what I wanted them to do.

"Don't stress. You'll get the hang of it."

What if I don't?

"Easy for you to say. You've had your whole life to deal with this." I set the pile of pins onto a wooden shelf in the dressing room.

Beck's hands flew to his mouth as his eyes roamed over my scantily clad body. "Holy shit. You look amazing. What did I tell you?"

My face flamed. I had completely forgotten about the cat suit. Turning back into the mirror, I had only one thought.

"It does look good, huh?" I agreed, meeting Beck's gaze in the reflection.

His expression was smug; he was clearly very pleased with himself. "You look fabulous. Brooklyn, eat your heart out. I can't believe you're dating Torent Stark."

I chewed on my lip. "We're not dating."

He pressed his lips together to keep from smirking. "If you say so."

CHAPTER 15

*M*om and Gigi were sitting on the porch swing, sipping hot apple cider as they waited for the trick-or-treaters to come by. The whole house smelled like cinnamon and apples. I snuck a quick glass of cider, crammed down a piece of pumpkin bread with butter, and then walked down the hall in my cat suit, equipped with ears and all.

Outside, the trees swayed with the wind as it blew through, shaking the branches. Leaves of deep orange, flaming red, and honey yellow spun as they danced to the ground, blanketing the grass in color. Someone in the neighborhood was burning leaves, the smell drifting through the trees. Autumn in Havenwood Falls was in full swing.

A part of me missed being a kid, going out around the neighborhood and eating so much candy I nearly puked.

"Why are you dressed like that?" Mom asked, getting up from the swing to refill the half-empty bowl of candy for the little kids.

Gigi smiled at me beside her. "The Haunting on Main Street is tonight."

"They still do that?" Mom asked, surprised.

"Every year. It's tradition," Gigi replied.

"Can't break tradition," I said, grabbing a Kit Kat from the black bucket shaped like a witch's cauldron.

Mom pursed her lips. "Promise me you'll be careful. Halloween in Havenwood Falls isn't your normal holiday. "

I rolled my eyes. "All the freaks come out at night. I got it."

She flicked one of my cat ears. "I don't think you do, but you will."

"What your mom is trying to say is, it's a powerful time of the year. The veil between the living and the dead is at its thinnest," Gigi explained.

Torent's Jeep pulled up before either of them could get into any more detail about the dead. The sight of his Jeep sent my heart racing.

"Is that the Stark boy?" Gigi asked. "You've been spending quite a lot of time with him."

"She has?" Mom queried, raising a brow. "A demon, Mallory? Really?"

I shrugged. "We're friends. Let's not make a big deal about it." I waved to Mom and Gigi as I walked off the porch. "Don't wait up," I called over my shoulder.

The car was filled with the tantalizing scent of Torent, and I couldn't stop myself from inhaling.

"Nice costume."

I let my eyes roam over him. "What are you supposed to be?"

He blinked, letting his gold demon eyes overtake the purple. "A demon."

"Clever," I said dryly. "If I knew dressing up was optional, I would never have let Beck talk me into this."

"Remind me to thank him later." He winked.

I punched him lightly in the shoulder. "Mom and my grandma are keeping a keen eye on you."

The Jeep slowly rolled out of the driveway. "I'm actually shocked your grandmother lets me on her property."

"Why is that?"

"I figured my family's reputation would be enough to have her warn you away. My brothers have only darkened my family's already tarnished name. One of my brothers, Brysen, has been banned from

Havenwood Falls by the Court for going full demon in public. Hence he is away at college. The other, Zaren, spent more time in the principal's office than the principal."

I fought the urge to move closer to him in the car, or reach out and run my hands along his flawless jawline. So I clasped my hands together in my lap to keep me from doing something reckless. But damn if I wasn't in the mood to break some rules. Maybe it was the eeriness of Halloween. Or being trapped inside a small space with a guy I hadn't been able to get out of my head since I stepped foot inside Havenwood Falls. But regardless, I was amped up.

"And you're the angel in your family."

He snorted. "Hardly, crash car. We're on our way to break into Brooklyn's house. What does that tell you?"

I dropped my head on the back of the seat. "How did I let you talk me into this?"

Torent flashed me his dimples. "Because I'm cute. And irresistible."

He might be right on all accounts, but this was insane. "You're sure no one will be home?"

"Her parents are working, and Brooklyn will be at the party. Beck is going to text us when she arrives, and then we'll be in the clear. Once we search her room and get the ring, we'll make an appearance at the party." He had it all figured out.

Brooklyn lived only a few blocks from my house, something that didn't make me feel comfortable. Torent killed his headlights as we turned down her street, parking off to the side of her house.

He twirled a lock of my hair around his finger.

"Your Catwoman costume is perfect for what we're about to do," he murmured huskily, his bright gaze holding mine.

I couldn't take my eyes off him, and that urge to be near him quadrupled. I leaned closer, our noses brushing, and for a moment, I wasn't sure if we were going to kiss or get out of the car. From the flecks of gold swimming in his eyes, I was leaning toward lots of bone-melting kissing.

Releasing my hair, he sighed. "You're making it very hard to concentrate."

My lips twitched. "Good."

It was another prolonged moment before he sighed. "It's time for your inner bad girl to shine. Keep to the shadows and try not to activate anything metal."

I rolled my eyes. "If you wanted someone stable as a sidekick, you should have brought Beck."

"Yeah, but he isn't nearly as hot."

I snorted.

We crept up the lawn, sticking to the pine trees. A group of kids passed on the sidewalk, not giving us a second glance. Torent slipped his hand in mine, and for once, I didn't object, but then the sparks of light began to swirl between us.

"We're really going to need to work on your magnetic energy," he whispered, grinning. "We can't have the air glowing every time we touch."

"It takes two to tango," I whispered back. The lights were a product of our joined powers.

"Touché."

Torent guided us to the back of the soft-blue Victorian-style house. All the windows were dark, and I took that as a good sign. I couldn't believe I was doing this. I was an accessory to burglary. How would that look on my college applications if we got caught? My chest squeezed, the beginnings of a panic attack rising within me.

Flattening his palms on the glass pane, he started to wedge the window upward. Taking a quick peek over his shoulder at me, he halted.

"Hey, it's going to be okay," he assured me. "I won't let anything happen to you."

I gazed into his eyes, and a warmth of calm washed through me.

"I'll be in and out so fast, you won't even know I'm gone," he said, trying to put me at ease.

That was unlikely. Somehow I was positive his absence would definitely affect me, but I nodded, leaning against the house while he opened the window wider. He boosted himself up and had one leg inside when my phone started singing.

Shit. Shit. Shit.

Taylor Swift belted from the little speakers, sounding in the silent woods like a bullhorn. I fumbled with my phone, scrambling to turn off the volume.

Torent turned and gave me a dull glare.

Okay. Fine. So I was the world's worst criminal. Sue me.

"Sorry," I whispered. "It's Beck." My eyes scanned over the text.

Abort mission. She's wearing the ring.

Could this night go any more wrong? I tugged on Torent's shirt, pulling him out of the window. "We have a problem. The ring is not in there."

"What are you talking about?"

I flipped my phone around, showing Beck's text.

He rubbed at the back of his neck as his eyes scanned the lit-up screen. "Damn."

"Now what?" I asked, my tone shrieky from the sudden increase in anxiety coursing through my veins.

"I was never good at plans. Come on." He grabbed my hand, leading me away from the house. "We're going to the party."

"She is never just going to hand it over."

"No, but I have many skills. You never know when sleight of hand might come in handy."

I should have known it would be something disreputable. "Are all your skills of a nefarious nature?"

He chuckled, and I took that as a yes.

CHAPTER 16

The celebration on Main Street was at the height of activity. Glowing jack-o'-lanterns were scattered throughout the square. White sheets hung as ghosts in the trees. Spider webs covered the shop windows.

After maneuvering his Jeep around the crowds and parking the car, Torent and I walked down the side alley, toward the sounds of Halloween. Our feet shuffled through the fallen leaves strewn over the street.

"We need to find Beck," I said, rushing to match my strides with Torent's long ones. It wasn't going to be easy, with everyone dressed up.

Just as we were about to cut around a corner, from the shadows emerged a body. I'd never been one for haunted houses or jump scares, and the sight of those glowing eyes coming straight for us had my internal girly shrill rising.

Torent caught the sound of my scream with this hand.

"Shh." His gaze caught mine, forcing me to focus on his face. "It's just Beck."

What? I took another look as a grinning Beck strolled up to me. "God, you scared me," I told Beck.

"So what's the plan? How are we going to get the ring back?" Beck asked.

"We should split up, cover more ground. You go with Beck, and if you see her, text me. You don't confront her alone." Torent gave me a pointed look, waiting for me to answer.

Beck ran a hand through his messy blue hair. "Should we really split up?"

Torent turned to Beck. "You got a better idea?"

"None that wouldn't piss off the Court," he mumbled.

Torent faced me, his hands framing my face. "Promise me you're not going to do anything without me."

He was really worried, which gave me the warm fuzzies, but it also only made the trepidation inside me triple. "Okay, fine. I won't do anything irrational."

Beck and I headed in the opposite direction, and I got an up-close view of the Haunting on Main Street. Strands of glittering lights were strewn in the trees and around the gazebo. The fountain was lit up in purple and orange. Hay bales, pumpkins, and other spooky decorations were hung around the square as speakers pumped the Halloween classics. It was both magical and ghoulish.

We passed a group of superheroes, ghosts, and little princesses as my heels clattered over the brick pavers.

"What was she wearing?" I asked, thinking it would be easier to spot Brooklyn if I knew what to look for. We turned a corner and halted in our steps. "Brooklyn," I said, squinting against the streetlight. "I've been looking for you." Wow. That was easier than I anticipated.

Static crackled in the air, making the hairs on my arms shoot up. She was alone, Leena and Cora not in sight. It was weird seeing her without her two sidekicks.

"Well, you found me," she snarled, her long hair framing her face.

My eyes adjusted, zeroing in on the ring. It sat on her finger, the garnet stone glowing in the dark. Even as I stared at it, I could feel the magnetic pull of its darkness. My hand twitched, dying to touch it, but something about Brooklyn stopped me from ripping it off her finger, a tingle of caution.

She was dressed up as a . . .

A groan escaped my lips.

Brooklyn and I were wearing the exact same outfit. Could this night get any worse?

The answer was yes.

I lifted my phone, but before I had the chance to unlock the screen, Brooklyn snatched it out of my hand, throwing it to the ground.

I stared in shock as the screen cracked, pieces of my phone scattering over the ground.

"What the hell, Brooklyn?" Beck growled. "You just broke her phone."

As I glared into her stormy eyes, I comprehended how much trouble we were in. Something was just not right about them.

"You and I need to have a little chat," she said, taking a step toward me.

Crap on a broomstick.

"Go get Torent," I ordered Beck.

He didn't immediately take off, and I knew he was struggling with the idea of leaving me alone with the she-devil.

"Go!" I hissed. "And hurry. I'll be fine."

He took off, bolting down the alley.

"Love the costume, by the way." I was being a smart-ass, but she deserved it. "I see you helped yourself to my ring as well. I'm shocked it fits."

She looked down at her hand admiringly. "That's the wonderful thing about magical objects. They have a way of forming to their owner."

"Yeah, well, the thing is, I sort of need it back."

Her response was to throw a bolt of electric energy at me. It hit the brick wall just to the right of my face. Wow. I wasn't expecting her to go all commando on me. We'd been in a minor scrap before, but this was different. This time, there was murder in her eyes, and she had delivered a warning. If I didn't listen, she would make this difficult for both of us.

112

I scrambled to put distance between us. *Just keep her rambling until Beck and Torent get back. How hard can that be?*

"Hold up a minute. Why don't we talk this through?" I said, walking backward. My back hit a brick wall. *Shit.* "Isn't there a no magic rule or something?"

She stalked toward me like a nymph on crack. "You don't even know who you are or what you're capable of."

And no doubt Brooklyn would enlighten me.

"True, but I don't think you need to get bent out of shape about it." Wrong answer.

The air charged again with Brooklyn's electric powers. Shocking was her specialty, and I wasn't keen on finding out how many volts she could shoot into my body.

"Do you think it was a coincidence you found this?" She raised her hand. "It called *you* because it recognized the darkness inside you."

Confusion set in. "What are you talking about?"

She lunged at me, suddenly in my face. Her fingers traced the line of my neck over the rapidly pulsing vein. "You're a descendant of Styx."

I flinched. "And?"

This wasn't a newsflash to me.

She let out a short hysterical laugh, her hand wrapping around my throat. "I can't believe they still haven't told you." Energy crackled over her knuckles. "What your family has kept hidden is that you have darkness inside you. You're dangerous."

That was funny, coming from her, and I hated that inside me, a bell of truth rang. I didn't want to believe her, but I knew my family was keeping secrets.

"You lie," I wheezed, my hands frantically trying to pry her fingers loose.

She slammed my head back against the wall, and black dots swirled behind my eyes. "Do I? You inherited it from your father. It is his darkness that runs in your veins and, combined with the shadows of your nymph powers, makes you unstable."

"Why do you care so much?"

Something other than hate flickered in her dark blue eyes. Sadness? Fear? "Before you showed up, I had my goddess's blessing."

I swallowed hard. "I don't know what that means."

The hatred was back, shining in her eyes, bolder and brighter than before, and for a heartbeat, I thought she might kill me. "My abilities have diminished. Your awakening drained some of mine, weakening my goddess, but strengthening Styx. Your coming back here has reinforced the bloodline and made her more powerful. You took the only thing that mattered from me."

I shook my head. "I swear I didn't do it on purpose. I'm sure we can fix it."

Her laugh was harsh. "You can't really be that stupid. No one tells a goddess to do anything."

Okay. That was it. I'd had enough. I didn't really want to hurt her, but I had to get the ring before it made Brooklyn do something she could never take back.

Lifting my arm, I slammed my elbow into her nose. Blood immediately began to ooze from her nostril. "No one calls me stupid and gets away with it. Now give me the ring before I'm forced to kick your ass."

She took the back of her hand and smeared the red sticky stuff from her face. "This is about to get fun."

Hell no, it wasn't.

Brooklyn's hand snaked out, grabbing a fist full of my hair in the ever classic bitch-hair-pull maneuver. It was effective. I bit the inside of my lip as she spun me around.

"Brooklyn," I shrieked, fire scorching at my scalp. "Oh, my god. Do you hear yourself? Wake up. You're talking about murdering me. Listen to me. That ring is poisoning you. I know, you hate me, and I get it, but do you really want to ruin your life?"

"That night at the falls when I found you with Torent, stumbling upon this ring was a nice little surprise, and it's going to give me back what you stole from me."

"It's a dark artifact, not a magical matchmaker," I hissed between my teeth, assuming what she wanted was Torent.

Brooklyn looked at me as if she was going to strangle the ever-loving crap out of me. "I don't want the guy. I want your magic."

Imagine that. I opened my mouth to tell her she could have it if she gave up the ring, but I never got the chance.

"Let her go, Brooklyn," a dark voice growled.

Brooklyn spun at the sound of the voice we both recognized. I exhaled, relief pouring from me.

Torent stepped out of the shadows, his violet eyes burning bright with flecks of gold. "I don't want to hurt you."

Beck was standing beside him, his silver eyes luminous and a snarl erupting from his throat, letting a bit of the wolf within him out.

"You're taking her side?" Brooklyn sneered. "First my powers, then you. She's taken everything from me. Why shouldn't she pay?"

Torent's eyes grew gold, radiating in the dark alley like a blazing fire. "Is it worth going to jail for? Being banished by the Court—or worse?"

Her gaze faltered, and I knew I had to make a move or risk getting hurt. Worse yet, she would turn her rage on Torent. The idea of him in danger sent me into a tizzy.

The air shimmered around me in a halo as I let the source of my power build inside me. And then, I let it go. Truthfully, I had no idea what I was doing, which was the worst way to do magic. As the string on my control released, the garbage dumpster in the alley came sailing straight for Brooklyn and me.

"Mallory!" Torent screamed.

He moved like lightning, shooting toward me at blinding speed, and yet, time seemed to slow to an infinite crawl. His arms wrapped around my waist, hauling me out of the way as the dumpster flew past us and smacked into Brooklyn. The force of the metal box tossed her body like a rag doll in the air before she landed with a hard thwack to the ground.

I gasped, lifting my head and peering through strands of tangled hair. My fingers were tingling and my ears ringing with the sickening sounds of metal hitting flesh.

Holy smokes.

"Are you okay?" Torent whispered, his eyes searching over my face.

I leaned my head back against the brick wall and started to breathe again. What had I done?

"Is she okay? Tell me I didn't . . ." My voice trailed off. I couldn't bring myself to say the words. Horror pitted in my stomach.

Beck was crouched beside Brooklyn's unmoving form. He pressed two fingers to the side of her neck. "No, she's breathing."

In that case . . . "Get the ring, quickly, before she wakes up and becomes the Terminator again," I rushed in a panicked string, urging Torent to take action.

Moving to Brooklyn's side, Torent reached for the ring, but he hesitated, glowering at the dark artifact.

"What are you waiting for?" Beck hissed.

Torent picked up Brooklyn's hand, slowly withdrawing the ring. Tense lines etched at the corners of his lips. His gaze was glued to the ring as he rocked back on his heels, still crouched.

"Beck, stay with Brooklyn," he ordered. "We're turning this over to the Court tonight. It's caused enough problems."

That we could agree on.

Torent stood up, staring at the ring with such intensity it gave me pause. A fiery light swirled around his body—demon fire. His eyes were brighter than I'd ever seen them, glowing with a possessive desire. The look on his face frightened me.

And to think I thought the horror was over.

He had warned me once before of the temptation a ring like this would pose for a demon. Seeing it firsthand was not the same as being forewarned.

"Torent," I called his name, hoping to get his attention focused on me. It was a no go. A knot formed in my belly, rolling its way up into my chest. "Hey, it's me." I placed my hand on his forearm.

His lips morphed into a menacing scowl while his eyes flicked up, tracking my movements like a hawk. Such darkness shimmered in them.

I turned my hand palm side up. "I can take it. I should never have asked you to retrieve it."

Not a muscle moved, except for the one in his jaw. It tightened. Beck stood up, shifting his body to stand in front of me, eyeing Torent with unease.

The last thing I wanted was for Torent and Beck to get into a fight, but I didn't know how to stop it from happening. I needed to do something, because things just escalated.

Torent attacked.

CHAPTER 17

Swinging a fist toward Beck, Torent let out a growl that shook his chest. Beck sunk to the ground, narrowly missing being flung across the alley.

"She's mine," Torent said tightly.

In any other situation, this would have called for some serious eye rolling. Now was not the time to get possessive, but the ring had a way of bringing out the absolute worst in people. Dread pitted in my belly. *Now what?*

"No one is contesting your feelings. Why don't you give me the ring?" Beck attempted to reason with the demon.

"You have no idea who you're messing with, dog," Torent snapped.

And just like that, the two went at it. I could never imagine two guys fighting over me, and now that I was seeing it firsthand, I wanted to erase it from my memory. The sounds alone made me cringe. Fists. Bones. Flesh.

No more blood. No more fighting. I'd had enough.

I shot forward, putting myself in between them. "Stop! Enough!"

Neither of them listened to me. Shocker.

Because I was out of options, I used my powers. Again. I focused on two pipes running down the side of the building. They bent at my will, wrapping around Torent to keep him from killing Beck. It was clear who the seasoned fighter was.

Poor Beck.

I had to give my best friend credit. It took balls to go toe to toe with a demon.

Torent's eyes glowed that demon iridescent gold. I stepped up to him.

"I'm sorry," I rasped. "You left me no choice."

"I wouldn't have hurt you," he stressed, almost pleading with me to believe him.

"I know. This is my fault." The ring was clutched in his hand, and I didn't delude myself into thinking he was going to voluntarily hand it over. All I could think about was Smeagol petting his precious from *Lord of the Rings*. Fingers trembling, I took his hand and flipped it over. I kept my gaze fastened to his while I opened his fingers, meeting little resistance. He had meant what he said about not hurting me, and the knowledge made my heart patter.

He closed his eyes, fighting off the power of the ring over his demon. I quickly took the troublesome piece of jewelry and stuffed it into my bra. Torent relaxed his body, resting his head on the brick wall. Using the familiar tingles swimming in my blood, I removed the pipes holding him prisoner. He exhaled, opening his eyes, and I was relieved to see they were crystal violet. No traces of gold.

Beck was near, waiting to see what happened next. His body was alert. Torent nodded in his direction, before looking at me with regretful eyes. "I never would have—"

I stopped him before he could say any more. "It's okay." Any minute, Brooklyn would wake up with a killer headache. "We need to go." For real this time.

Torent ran a hand through his hair, eyes skating over Brooklyn. "City Hall isn't far."

Thank god. Not only was I dying for this night to end, I wanted to lose the boots. Padding down the alley, we left Beck with a stirring Brooklyn. He was going to have his hands full.

The Court of the Sun and the Moon had a secret entrance at the rear of City Hall. Torent knew how to reach someone who would know what to do with the Teardrop of Desire. All we had to do was get there without incident.

It sounded simple enough, but if there was one thing I'd learned about being supernatural, it was that nothing was as easy as it seemed when magic and the unknown were involved. This was my burden. I had been the one who had found the ring, who had unleashed its powers into Havenwood Falls. It was my duty to see it returned into the hands of the Court. I didn't know if I was skeptical or relieved that we managed to make our way across the square to City Hall without incident.

We skirted around to the back of the two-story building, and I tried not to dwell on what Brooklyn had said to me during her enchanted psychobabble, but my mind went there. What if she had been telling the truth? What if I inherited some kind of bad mojo from my father? I knew virtually nothing about him. And Mom and Gigi were definitely not telling me something.

Did I even want to know?

Would it be better if I went on living my life blessedly unaware? Would knowing give it power, bringing forth the darkness?

So many questions. So many uncertainties. So many possibilities.

"Are you sure you're okay?" Torent asked, interrupting my internal rant of panic.

I hadn't noticed the quickening of my breath until now and forced myself to take a deep, even amount of air. We were outside the rear of the building, and my palms had gone damp.

"I'm just ready to get rid of this thing." *And for my life to go back to normal*, I added inside my head. But that wasn't in the cards for me. Not anymore.

I was who I was. There was no running from it.

We paused at a door that looked like nothing more than a maintenance entrance, but the moon and mountain emblem situated above was the only indicator it was something more. This was where the governing body of Havenwood Falls met. It consisted of the leaders from the Old Families, the descendants of the town's founders.

I'd never been inside, but I could sense the air of magic that lived within.

Torent turned the handle and waited for me to walk through. I rubbed my hands over my arms, a tremble tickling my spine. We descended a flight of stairs into the City Hall basement and then through a long hallway that opened to a small reception area. It was there that Addie Beaumont, dressed as the sexiest *Star Wars* stormtrooper I'd ever seen, greeted us with her helmet in hand.

"Addie," Torent addressed her by name.

She smiled at him, the stone in her nose twinkling under the light. "What brings you to the Court on All Hallows' Eve of all nights? I was about to hit a party before duty calls at the witching hour." She gave us a wink.

Torent nodded toward me. *My turn.* I dug the ring out of my pocket and twirled it in my fingers.

"I came to bring the Court what I'm fairly certain is a magical relic." The ring was still in my hand, and now that I was here, I was finding it difficult to relinquish it from my possession.

Intrigue brightened in Addie's brown eyes, behind the black-framed glasses. "And how did you come across such an object?"

"At the bottom of Peacock Lake," I retorted.

She lifted a brow. "Let's see this relic."

I opened my palm, showing her the gold band with the crimson stone embedded. Its aura seemed to reach out to me, tempting me to slip it on.

Addie's eyes darkened as she stared intently. "You were right to bring this to the Court. The magic rooted to the ring is dark and powerful, and someone's been trying to collect magical artifacts, especially dark ones. It would be disastrous for our town if the Collector got his hands on this."

The bangles on her wrists jingled as she produced a small velvet-lined box out of thin air. My eyes followed hers to stare at the Teardrop of Desire.

"Mallory?"

It was Torent's silky voice that pulled me from the trance. I glanced up, meeting his worried gaze. Without risking another entrancement, I took a deep breath and picked up the ring, plunking it into the box.

A million pounds was lifted from my shoulders, and I would be happy if I never owned another ring in my life.

Addie quickly snapped the little box closed. "I'll make sure this gets kept somewhere safe. You don't have to worry about it anymore."

I nodded, feeling relieved that someone who was more capable than me had possession of the cursed ring.

"Thanks, Addie," Torent replied, slipping a hand to the small of my back. He applied the slightest pressure, guiding me to move. We'd done what we had set out to do. There was nothing left to say.

We walked back the way we came, climbing the stairs and slipping through the door. Outside, the world was still moving. A group of kids was passing by, laughing and unwrapping candy from their Halloween haul.

Strolling down the sidewalk beside the building, I snuck a peek at Torent, curious what was going through his head.

"That was fun," I stated sarcastically. "Next time you want to bring me to a party, remind me to—"

He moved so fast, I didn't have a chance to prepare myself. One second he was in front of me, and then suddenly he was kissing me as if he was starved for water. I had no choice but to respond, his lips pulling a response from mine.

My mouth parted in a gasp, and being the rogue that he was, Torent deepened the kiss. The cool metal piercing of his tongue brushed against mine, soothing the instant heat. It was a battle of cool and hot inside my mouth, and when he pulled away slowly, my lips clung to his, not ready to end the blissful torture. My hand was curved around the nape of his neck.

"Look." His eyes went upward, mine following. Northern lights lit up the dark alley in the most breathtaking sight.

I doubted I would ever get sick of seeing the electric display of lights.

"It's beautiful," I whispered, disentangling myself from him.

"We did this, together. Our powers, they complement each other —*we* complement each other."

So much for letting my heart rate return to normal—that stupid fluttering was back in my chest. I chewed on my lip. Maybe he was right. Or maybe I wanted him to be right, because my hormones were going batshit bonkers at the moment. "Thank you for saving my life."

"Anytime, crash car. What are boyfriends for?"

"You're not my boyfriend," I clarified, trying to convince myself as much as him . . . maybe more so.

"Really? The way you just kissed me says otherwise," he murmured with a slight curve to his lips.

Damn Torent and his dimples.

~

Thank you for reading!
Torent and Mallory's journey continues in
Ascending Darkness.

~

We hope you enjoyed this story in the Havenwood Falls High series of novellas featuring a variety of supernatural creatures. The series is a collaborative effort by multiple authors.

You may also enjoy these other books in the Young Adult Havenwood Falls High series:

The Fall by Kristen Yard
Forever Emeline by Katie M. John
Curse the Night by R.K. Ryals
Willful by Liz Ferry

Stay up to date at www.HavenwoodFalls.com

J.L. WEIL

ABOUT THE AUTHOR

USA Today bestselling author J.L. Weil lives in Illinois, where she writes teen & new adult paranormal romances about spunky, smart-mouth girls who always wind up in dire situations. For every sassy girl, there is an equally mouthwatering, overprotective guy. Of course, there is lots of kissing. And stuff.

An admitted addict to Love Pink clothes, raspberry mochas from Starbucks, and Jensen Ackles, she loves gushing about books and Supernatural with her readers.

She is the author of the international bestselling Raven & Divisa series.

www.jlweil.com

ACKNOWLEDGMENTS

I need to start by thanking Kristie Cook for letting me be a part of this amazing world and community she has created. I feel truly lucky to be one of the authors who gets to write in Havenwood Falls. You put your heart and soul into this project and it really shows.

A HUGE thank you to all the readers who have stuck with me!! It has been a crazy journey. I am so blessed to have such wonderful friends in this author world. Hugs!!

For my Dark Divas. I love you to death. Thank you so much for the best squad in the world. What would I do without you?!

AN EXCERPT

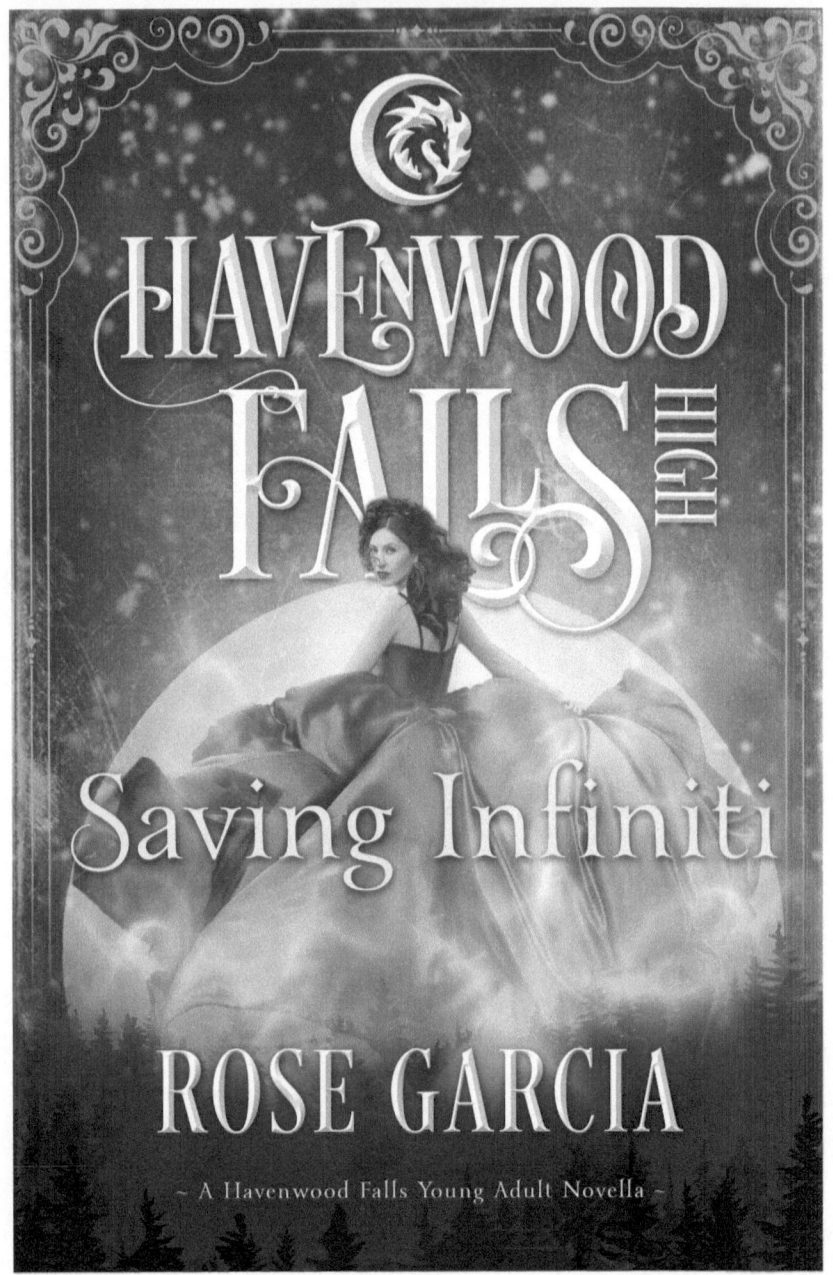

HAVENWOOD FALLS HIGH

Saving Infiniti

ROSE GARCIA

~ A Havenwood Falls Young Adult Novella ~

Saving Infiniti (A Havenwood Falls High Novella) by Rose Garcia

Welcome to Havenwood Falls, a small town in the majestic mountains of Colorado. A town where legacies began centuries ago, bloodlines run deep, and dark secrets abound. A town where nobody is what you think, where truths pose as lies, and where myths blend with reality. A place where everyone has a story. Including the high schoolers. This is only but one . . .

Infiniti Clausman is making the most of senior year. Throwing parties, pulling pranks, and breaking all the rules, she's determined to graduate with a bang! But there's one thing on her senior year bucket list she hasn't been able to cross off yet—falling in love. In fact, she's never even been kissed.

Infiniti hopes to change this when she travels from Houston to Colorado for the holiday break. Instead, she finds her world turned upside down when she discovers all things supernatural exist, time travel is real, and her very life is at stake. Suddenly, that kiss is the least of her worries.

Joe Greg will never forget the injured girl he and Kase Kasun found on the side of the mountain. It was 2012, and he was only twelve, but the image of the wreckage and his interaction with the girl has never left him. When he sees the girl again in 2018, she looks exactly the same. He figures out that she's time-traveled to his present, with a reaper on her heels and a mystery to unravel. Drawn to protect her, he's hell-bent on standing by her side. Even if it means his death.

SAVING INFINITI

Fleet ran his fingers through his dark hair before tilting his head toward the night sky. He eyed the top floor of the Houston skyscraper Tavion had called home since tracking Dominique and her protectors to the oversized Texas city. A cool December breeze swept through the streets, kicking up the stench of trash from a nearby dumpster. Fleet hated all the concrete, all the glass buildings, but mostly he hated taking on the role of being one of the Tainted and on Tavion's side against the Pures. He had accepted the directive for the greater good, but the passing of so many years had started to muddle allegiances in his brain. All sense of right and wrong had started to merge. Too good at his job, he found himself alone and sure of nothing but the perpetual clench in his gut.

Fleet closed his eyes. He tried not to picture the horrible things he had done in Tavion's name while tracking Dominique, but had a hard time suppressing the images. His only solace was knowing that in this life, her final life, Dominique had no recollection of any of her prior lives. Even if it meant forgetting him forever, Fleet hoped Dominique's memories would never return. There was too much pain and suffering for anyone to have to recall, let alone someone he secretly cared about.

Fleet banged his fist against the glass wall of the downtown apartment building. "Get your shit together, man."

Pressing his palm against the cool surface, he held his breath, then let it trickle out between clenched teeth. He had built a brick wall around his true feelings for Dominique and the Pures ages ago, vowing not to let anyone ever see that side of himself, especially Tavion. He had a job to do and was determined to see it through no matter what. To hell with what anyone thought of him.

"Don't let anyone in," he muttered, while strengthening the fortress of his mind. With his vulnerabilities hidden, he turned his focus to Tavion's directive: find Dominique and prepare her for death.

"I got this," he whispered to himself. "I can do this."

With his emotions in check, he jerked the heavy door open. He nodded at the security guard behind the holiday-adorned lobby desk. The guard peered at him from over his computer screen.

"Hey, Fleet. Your boss is in quite a mood tonight." He whistled. "Quite a mood."

Fleet knew exactly what sort of mood Tavion was in. Starving for death and destruction, he displayed hatred like a neon sign. But some days his harsh light shone brighter than usual. Today must have been one of those days.

"Thanks, Sammy."

Sammy said something else about Christmas spirit and holiday joy, but Fleet ignored him. Joy didn't exist for him, hadn't in a long time. And it wasn't likely to ever return.

Pushing the button for the top floor with his key card, Fleet repeated his mission over and over in his mind, drowning out the doubt that lingered in the darkest corners. With a ding, the steel doors opened. He loathed interacting with Tavion and mostly operated on his own, but every now and again Tavion would call him in for a status report.

Fleet steadied himself. He cleared his mind. He stepped into the all-white foyer of the sprawling penthouse. Thick silence and heavy foreboding sucked the air right out of the space. He knew this meeting, like all the others, was going to suck.

Windows lined the long L-shaped living space that looked out on the sparkling buildings of the massive city. The dark sky outside blended in with the shadowy room. Only the soft light from the gleaming neighboring structures gave any indication of life in the space. An oversized brown leather chair facing the view was the lone piece of furniture in the entire apartment. It was Tavion's favorite spot.

Tavion extended his arm over the armrest. He waved Fleet over. "Come."

Fleet's boots thudded against the marble floors, the echo of each step bouncing all around him like a lonely symphony. He took his place next to Tavion and clasped his hands behind his leather jacket. Glancing at Tavion, he saw that he was dressed in his usual black suit. His profile revealed a deep scowl.

"How may I help you, sir?"

Tavion moved his long skeletal fingers to his pale face and started rubbing his chin. "Dominique Wells," he said, letting the *s* trickle out of his mouth as if he were a slithering snake. "I've been thinking of her final life, and the differences here as compared to our other lives, and I do not like it. The events of late do not sit well with me. This year in particular, 2012, is fraught with too many unknowns."

Fleet remembered a time when Tavion's appearance was hardy and robust. Tavion had once stood on the side of right, but over time, a deep-seated hatred toward mankind pulled him away. Tavion detested humans and blamed them for the gradual destruction of the natural world. His departure split the Transhumans into two factions: the good became known as the Pure. The evil became known as the Tainted, and Tavion became their leader. He eventually marked Dominique for death in an attempt to get back at the Pure. With each passing decade, Tavion's hate grew in his heart and in his body, reducing him to his current death-like appearance.

Yet Fleet knew Tavion was right. Things in this life were way different, mainly with the involvement of first lifers Trent Avila and Infiniti Clausman. Friends of Dominique's, Fleet suspected they'd play a role in Dominique's quest for survival. It seemed Tavion shared the same sentiment.

Testing his theory, Fleet asked, "What do you mean?"

Tavion let out a low growl. "Do not pretend that you know not of what I speak." He stood and faced Fleet. "Or are you keeping something from me?"

Hiding his surprise at the threatening move, Fleet eyed Tavion with matching menace, a look he knew Tavion respected. Tavion resided in perpetual paranoia, forcing Fleet to work overtime to keep Tavion's trust secured.

Fleet raised his chin. "I assure you, I am not keeping anything from you, sir. Nor would I make pretense."

Fleet waited for Tavion's response, wondering if Tavion had somehow discovered the conflict within him. Fleet curled his fingers behind his back, ready to form an energy ball and strike Tavion if needed. Luckily, Tavion's face softened. He placed his hand on Fleet's shoulder.

"My apologies, Fleet. I should not be so angry with you, especially since you are the only one I've been able to count on all these very long years."

Fleet relaxed his fist, but his body remained tense. "It's okay, sir."

Tavion eased back down on his chair. He returned his gaze to the twinkling lights of the downtown buildings. "Dominique keeps eluding us, but I know she's close. I can feel her fear, can practically smell her blood. Her parents cannot hide her forever. Eventually there'll be another break, and we'll find her. In the meantime, I want you to follow this one."

Tavion let loose a dark mist from his palm. It gathered into a swirl, forming a large oval shape. The mist thinned out, revealing an image of Infiniti Clausman, Dominique's neighbor and friend. Petite with small features and long dark hair, she danced around her room while packing a suitcase.

"This first lifer is important," Tavion said. "I can sense it."

Just as Fleet suspected, she *was* important. He thought of the other first lifer.

"What of Trent Avila?"

"Leave him to me." Tavion jabbed his finger at the floating image. "But this one is leaving in the morning with her mother on a holiday trip, and I want you on her heels. You will follow her to Colorado. I want to know everything about her. Understood? What she eats, what she drinks, what she loves, what she fears. All of it."

By the look of her room and the way she carried herself, she seemed like an average teenager of the time—interested in parties, music, and all things superficial. Yet something about her had struck a chord with Tavion. Fleet, too. There had to be more to her, but what?

"Understood, sir."

Tavion whisked the image away. He dismissed Fleet with a wave. "Go."

A sinking feeling grew in the pit of Fleet's stomach as he rode the elevator down to the first floor. He'd never been away from Dominique before. He didn't want to risk Tavion finding her while he was gone, yet he also didn't want Tavion to know about the conflict within him. Should he abandon Tavion's directive? Or should he follow Infiniti to Colorado and trust that Dominique would not be found until he returned?

Back outside, Fleet paced up and down the sidewalk, his mind on overdrive. Everything had repeated perfectly from lifetime to lifetime, but in this life nothing was the same. Nothing! And it was driving him crazy.

"It's better that way," a small voice said.

Fleet whipped around and saw a young girl. No more than five years old, she wore a long white dress that matched her long hair. She studied him with oversized green eyes.

"What's better?" he asked.

"That everything is different in this life."

A million things raced through Fleet's mind. Before he could say anything, the girl went on.

"You need to follow her. She will need you."

"The first lifer?"

"Yes. Infiniti. She will need you in Colorado."

A pink shimmery hue radiated from her body. Recognizing the young girl as part of the spirit world, yet sensing something familiar about her, he peered at her with questioning eyes. He moved closer.

"Who are you?"

The girl lifted her skirt off the floor with dainty hands and gave an old-fashioned curtsey. "I am Abigail. It's nice to meet you." Her innocent face flashed with remorse. "I used to be like you, but then I died. I had to in order to help save Dominique. Her friend is my friend, and Infiniti is important. Everyone in this life is. So you see, that's why you need to follow her. You need to help her."

Fleet latched on to her statement about being like him, but had no idea what she meant. Before he could ask her to explain, she stepped forward. She held out her hand, as if she wanted to touch him, but then dropped her arm. She lowered her head, her shoulders sagged, and she looked as if she might burst into tears.

"I am so sorry about what you are going through. I really am."

He looked about to see if anyone was around to witness the conversation he was having with the spirit girl, but the streets were empty. When he turned back to Abigail, she was gone.

"Hey! Come back!"

Desperate to ask the girl more questions, he waited a few minutes for her to return, but she didn't. He clasped his hands behind his neck. He walked up and down the sidewalk. He had no idea what she meant about feeling sorry for him, but figured it had to do with him joining Tavion's ranks. Shit, even he felt sorry for himself. He eyed the night sky that had begun to lighten to a soft gray. If Infiniti was important enough to garner Tavion's attention, then she probably would need his help.

"Guess I'm going to Colorado."

Purchase *Saving Infiniti* where books are sold.